# dangerous decisions
# and hidden
# choices

Other titles in the Summit High series:

# dangerous decisions and hidden choices

# Matt Tullos
## with Tracey L. Bumpus

BROADMAN
& HOLMAN
PUBLISHERS

Nashville, Tennessee

© 1999
by Matt Tullos
All rights reserved
Printed in the United States of America

0-8054-1976-4

Published by Broadman & Holman Publishers, Nashville, Tennessee
Page Design: Anderson Thomas Design, Nashville, Tennessee
Typesetting: PerfecType, Nashville, Tennessee
Editorial Team: Vicki Crumpton, Janis Whipple, Kim Overcash

Dewey Decimal Classification: F
Subject Heading: HIGH SCHOOLS—FICTION
Library of Congress Card Catalog Number: 99-38100

Scripture quotations are from the Holy Bible, New International Version, copyright ©
1973, 1978, 1984 by International Bible Society.

**Library of Congress Cataloging-in-Publication Data**
Tullos, Matt, 1963–
    Dangerous decisions and hidden choices / Matt Tullos.
    p.   cm. — (Summit High series ; bk. 5)
    Summary: Clipper relies on his Christian faith as he and his friends at Summit
High struggle with issues involving sexual harassment, premarital pregnancy, and
how best to respond to a bomb threat.
    ISBN 0-8054-1976-4
    [1. Friendshiip Fiction.  2. Christian life Fiction.  3. High Schools Fiction.
4. Schools Fiction.]  I. Title.  II. Series: Tullos, Matt, 1963– Summit High series ; 5.
PZ7.T82316Dan       1999
[Fic]—dc21

                                     99-38100
                                       CIP

1 2 3 4 5  03 02 01 00 99

# Dedication

To Nathan

Clipper Hayes entered the crowded lobby of the Radisson Hotel. "If you ask me, this is no political debate; it's a shmooze-fest." He studied the well-dressed crowd of mainly forty-some-thing men and women. "I love the smell of Scope in the evening."

"Looks like all the network affiliates are here—FOX, NBC, CBS, Nickelodeon, Animal Planet . . . " Justin Henderson said smiling.

Autumn Sanders' eyes darted to the ceiling as she prayed aloud, "God, why did I think it was a good idea to bring these guys with me?"

"Hey look! Free food!" Clipper said as a waiter in a tuxedo passed by with a tray of hors d'oeuvres.

"Clipper, forget the food. Just settle back and relax," pleaded Autumn. "You don't want to make a spectacle of yourself."

"But—" Clipper said quickly.

"Get some food. Fine. But please, when I received passes to this debate, there *was* a no-pets-allowed clause in it," Autumn said only half-joking.

Autumn, Justin, and Clipper were by far the youngest attendees of the Republican State Senatorial Debate. Autumn received an invitation after she won a political essay contest a few weeks earlier. It was for her and two guests and included a meal and priority seating for this televised town-hall-style debate. When Autumn received the invitation, she offered the other two passes to her parents, but they had a previous commitment. Kandi Roper, her best friend, also couldn't attend. She had a research paper deadline looming over her, so she opted out. That left Clipper and Justin—the odd couple with big appetites who seemed to be in more-obnoxious-than-average moods.

The three tried to blend in with the high-society types as they stood by a lace-covered table that held elegant coffee cups and saucers. "So Justin," Clipper began, "you Republican or Democrat?"

"I'm kind of a third-party guy, I guess," Justin replied nonchalantly. He waved at a tall man standing solemnly in the corner, wearing an earpiece. His black suit was nondescript and he moved further back against the wall when Justin waved. "So, Autumn, you think that guy over there is like security or secret service or what?"

"What guy?"

"The guy who's doing a James Bond over there next to the doorway."

Autumn exhaled loudly, somewhat exasperated, "I don't know. Let's head on in and get a seat."

Autumn was a sixteen-year-old African-American student and accustomed to being in the minority. This Republican town meeting was no exception. That disappointed her, but she didn't dwell on it. She tried not to let racial issues intimidate her or slant her perspectives.

Justin and Clipper were seniors at Summit High School. They had grown up together, but the foundation of their friendship with Autumn was their faith. Still, from outward appearances, Clipper, Autumn, and Justin were a strange threesome. Justin had buzzed brown hair and a muscular physique. Clipper, on the other hand, stood about five inches taller and was skinny, with long, shaggy, reddish hair, and feet that made his shoes look like skis.

After the audience moved into the ballroom, the moderator of the debate, Governor Jenkins, stepped to the platform, and the audience broke into applause.

"Good evening and welcome to this town meeting brought to you by the Republican Party of Indiana. We're very proud this debate is being broadcast throughout central Indiana with the help of the local public television station. It is also my honor to introduce the two worthy Republican candidates for this district: incumbent Rob Lindsay and his opponent, James Cleary."

Autumn knew about Rob Lindsay from his tough stance against government spending. He had been the target of a brutal campaign a few years back but had held on to win re-election. But she knew nothing of James Cleary. He appeared to be in his midthirties, much younger than Lindsay, who had to be sixty years old or older. Cleary had a confident—even contagious—smile, light brown hair, and dark eyes that complemented his dark green paisley tie. To Autumn, he seemed more *GQ* than political.

Throughout the debate, it became obvious to Autumn and probably most of the audience that Cleary, the lesser-known underdog, had the upper hand. His answers were straightforward and less defensive. He seldom used his notes and looked directly into the eyes of his audience, occasionally shifting his eyes toward the camera, a debating tactic not lost on Autumn.

"When's this thing gonna be over?" Clipper asked Autumn under his breath.

"I don't know, Clipper. Be patient," Autumn whispered in a motherly tone.

"I mean, great food but—"

"Clipper!" Autumn whispered, her teeth clinched.

"Is this what my pledge to PBS is going for? I knew I'd be supporting *Sesame Street* and *Barney* but—"

Autumn didn't have to say anything. Her sudden glare said it for her—shut up!

As Senator Lindsay droned on about budgeting restraint and the need for a new tax code, Autumn tried to ignore Clipper's faint whispers to Justin.

"This thing's been going on for over an hour now," Clipper whined. "I thought they had time limits for these deals. The problem is that these people keep asking questions. If everybody would just clam up, we could get back to the free food."

Autumn knew what she was about to do wouldn't be a popular maneuver with her two bored guests, but she couldn't restrain herself. She put her hand in the air as Cleary finished answering a question.

"Hey, Autumn, I couldn't help but notice that your right hand just went up," Clipper said.

Autumn ignored him.

"Really! It's up in the air. Look at it." Clipper said again, but got quiet fast as the floor moderator brought the wireless hand-held microphone over to their row.

"We have another question from the audience," the moderator said as he gestured toward Autumn. "Tell us your name."

Autumn stood. Up to that moment, she had felt no anxiety at all. But when the camera panned toward her and she held the microphone, she thought her heart might bounce out of her chest. Thanks to her debate experience, she hid her anxiety well. "My name is Autumn Sanders, and I'm a student at Summit High School here in Indianapolis," she began. "Senator Lindsay, I have heard you speak in the past about adding more funds for law enforcement, but what positive steps will you take to curb violence in our public schools?"

Senator Lindsay paused momentarily, looking a bit surprised by the poise of this young audience member. "I think," Lindsay began carefully, "my record speaks for itself."

"How so?" returned Autumn. "With all due respect to you, Senator, you voted against bills that protect students from acts of violence on campuses. Specifically, you voted against funding for on-campus law enforcement."

"I think you are mistaken young lady," countered Senator Lindsay. "We have to weigh the cost and impact of these proposed programs. Allow me to clarify. I believe that pouring more money into a plan that is flawed from its inception is wrong."

"How were these plans flawed?" Autumn asked. Suddenly this polite town meeting had an air of excitement. People in the audience in front of her turned to see who she was. Adrenaline pulsed through her body. Out of the corner of her eye she could see herself on the TV monitor, but she didn't skip a beat.

Lindsay's eyebrows raised as he began to answer. "I, along with a number of my colleagues, felt that it was best to spend funds in law enforcement in other ways. Besides, violence on high school campuses is down 53 percent from last year," he concluded with a smile.

"I think you are referring to the recent report in *Time* magazine," Autumn continued. "But that figure is a national figure. Do you have any idea what the numbers are in Indianapolis?"

Suddenly the senator's eyes were like those of a sixth grader who hadn't done his homework. "Well," he said hesitantly, "I don't have those figures. I mean, not off the top of my head. But—"

"According to a recent study, acts of violence increased 38 percent last year in Indianapolis. I know you might think that I'm just a high school student. I'm underaged. I can't vote. But I would hope that our fellow citizens would be able to elect representatives and senators who will look out for *my* future. I shouldn't have to get up in the morning wondering if one of my classmates or I will be threatened at gunpoint or be the target of some violent extremist. I would hope that the Republican party would make it a priority to protect us. I also hope that when we pray outside our school, we can do so without having one eye open for fear of an act of violence."

The audience broke into thunderous applause, which left both candidates scrambling to put a positive spin on her passionate statement.

Justin yelled over the applause, "You go, girl!"

In her room, lit only by the glow of the computer monitor, Kandi Roper ran the spell check on her research paper: "The Cold War: Futility or Freedom." She resented the time this project had stolen from her, but she felt relieved and even proud of finishing it. She clicked on her journal and wrote:

*11:45 P.M. September 18*

*Finally concluded THE PAPER. Yes!*

*I'm exhausted. My fingers sting. My eyes burn. So why am I still typing? Sometimes I feel like major projects aren't really done until I write about them in my journal. I guess I'm a little compulsive. Clipper, the king of spontaneity, would say I'm way beyond compulsive. In some ways I missed being with Autumn, Clipper, and Justin tonight, and in other ways it was nice to just go into hiding for a little while. I really don't know what's going on with Justin and me lately. For some reason we just aren't clicking. I feel like he's become more of a big brother than a romantic interest. I don't know how that happened. We have just had some really petty arguments lately. I really do care for him, but sometimes—*

A chime indicating she had new E-mail interrupted Kandi's thoughts. *Probably junk E-mail,* she thought. But when she clicked on her mail icon she found a message from Luke Ellis, the president of the Fellowship of Christian Students at Summit.

*Dear friends,*

*As you know, our annual "See You at the Pole" event is just around the corner. We need to be praying about our involvement. Yesterday, I received a very disturbing anonymous threat. A few others have received these threats also. I honestly don't know what to do except pray about our involvement, and I wanted to ask you to pray too. Jesus didn't promise that we'd have an easy road when we live the life He taught, so we shouldn't see this as a sign that we should withdraw. Maybe we could pray somewhere else or just take a step back and allow the police to check into it. I don't want to scare you, but I felt all of you should know about this.*

*In Christ,*
*Luke*

Outside a bar across town, well beyond the glow of the neon signs that hung in the window, two guys sat on the hood of a blue Camaro. The light of a match briefly interrupted the darkness as one of them lit a cigarette.

"If the deal goes down, you're going to have to promise me that it'll be buildings, not people. Understand? You don't want an Oklahoma City situation."

"I just want to give 'em a good scare."

"This should definitely do the trick."

"Are you sure this will work?"

"It was tested over the summer. If you have the right instructions and the right ingredients, it's as easy as baking a cake."

"When can we get it?"

"If you've got the cash, I've got the trash."

"They scared?"

"What do you think?"

Kandi stepped out of her car at Summit High the next morning and heard a vaguely familiar voice call her name.

She turned around and saw Eli Waller, an athlete whom she had talked to once or twice in passing. She had an idea what he wanted; he had recently met Autumn and almost immediately fell for her.

"Do you remember me?" Eli said as he walked up to her. His six-foot-five-inch frame dwarfed her. "We met in biology class last year."

"You're Eli."

"Right."

"And," Kandi said, carefully measuring her words, "you met Autumn at the sports banquet."

"She's been talking about me. Right? This is a good sign?" Eli asked hopefully.

"She's mentioned you, but you probably already know that she's a little embarrassed by—"

"Embarrassed by me?" Eli's expression was sad.

"Not embarrassed by you. I mean, she doesn't make a big deal about who she dates. That's the way she is."

"She said we went out on a date? That's also a good sign. I didn't really have any idea what she thought happened the other night. I mean, I wanted it to be a date, but have you ever been out with someone, and you really weren't sure if you were dating or just hanging? That's the way I felt.".

Kandi laughed, "Welcome to the twenty-first century."

"Did she say anything about it?" Eli asked.

"She just said the two of you went to the Jars of Clay concert the other night, and she had a good time."

"That's it?" Eli asked, somewhat disappointed.

"Look Eli, you'll have to understand that Autumn isn't really in a, well, a dating mindset. I'm surprised she even went out with you. I mean, no offense. She thinks you're a great guy and all that, but she has her boundaries. If she didn't want to go, she wouldn't. Period. But she's really focused on school and trying to get into a good college."

"I am too."

Kandi smiled and stopped at the door of the school. "Probably not the way she is, Eli. I don't think many people could be that focused."

Before Kandi could take another breath and finish her thought, someone above them yelled, "Hey, Eli!"

By the time they looked up, a huge pink globe fell from the sky. Before Kandi could move, the water balloon crashed onto her head. A guy with long, sandy-blond hair and an earring looked down at them from one of the classroom windows, wincing with regret.

Kandi froze, breathless, soaked, and totally shocked.

"Zack!" Eli said angrily. "What were you thinking?!"

A sheepish "Oops" was all Zack could muster as several students gathered around looking up at him. "Um . . . that was supposed to be for Eli," he said to them.

"You either need target practice or glasses," Eli said.

"Sorry," Zack said, his face twisted in embarrassment. He waved at Kandi. "Um . . . I'm Zack," he called down from the window, "Zack Galloway. I just moved here this summer."

Kandi shook her head and began walking back to her car, her arms wrapped around her shivering body.

"Guess you'll be going home to change," Eli said.

"You're smart, Eli, especially when it comes to your choice of friends," Kandi said sarcastically.

Clipper had also received the E-mail the night before from Luke about the possibility of canceling the "See You at the Pole" rally. As he thought about it all night, his mind kept returning to his encounter with A. C. a week ago. Clipper had initiated a friendship with A. C. the first week of school. Clipper was very sure that God wanted him to reach out to this outsider and tell him about God's love, but A. C. didn't appear open to even considering the possibility of a loving God. Life, to A. C., was meaningless and a dead-end journey. Clipper thought about his encounter with A. C. on Skull's Bluff. He remembered A. C.'s anger.

*"You don't have any reason to hate God," A. C. said as he pointed a gun at Clipper. "You didn't have a mom who left you on the doorsteps of your grandmother's house when you were six weeks old. You didn't have an alcoholic dad. That's my life in living color and surround sound. So if your God is real, then I have a reason to be pretty hacked off at Him." A. C. pulled back the trigger. "It's a tale told by an idiot."*

Clipper replayed the struggle as they wrestled for control of the gun, the sound of the trigger and the echo of the errant shot. He winced at the thought that the bullet could easily have lodged in the head of either one of them. He remembered the sudden blow to the head that left him momentarily unconscious, and then A. C.'s haunting letter filled with dark implications. It read:

*Every story has two sides. Remember that. I hope you'll do "the Christian thing" and leave me out of your story about what happened tonight. If you really care, you'll forget about all this. One thing I can say about you is that you really are persistent about your beliefs. And for some reason, you've zoned in on me. I don't understand it, but you've made me think. See you at school. Maybe we can debate without the use of deadly force.*

> *The skeptic,*
> *A. C.*

*Surely A. C. has heard about all of our "See You at the Pole" plans. Is he the one making the threats?* Clipper wondered. They hadn't talked since that violent night at Skull's Bluff, but after reading the E-mail from Luke, he had to somehow, some way, find out if A. C. had anything to do with the threats.

After lunch the next day, Clipper got his chance to talk to A. C. He saw him alone on one of the concrete benches outside the school, staring straight ahead at the traffic about a hundred yards away. When Clipper approached him, A. C. didn't even glance at him. He just kept staring vacantly ahead. Clipper could tell from the scent of marijuana that A. C. wouldn't be learning much the rest of the day at school. As he walked over and sat down next to A. C., Clipper mouthed an inaudible prayer: *Help me.*

A. C. greeted Clipper without even looking at him. "You sure are persistent. I thought for sure you'd get the point by now," he said, and then laughed lightly.

"I think I got your point loud and clear. I've still got the bruises to prove it. I don't agree with it, though. I think you're making a mistake," Clipper replied.

"What mistake? My whole life is made up of mistakes. Which mistake are you referring to?"

"About God. You've got a huge chip on your shoulders. I might have one too if I'd been through all you've been through," Clipper admitted.

"Is that why you came over here? To preach?" A. C. asked, his eyes still focusing on the traffic.

"I'm not preaching," Clipper's voiced raised in frustration.

"Could have fooled me," A. C. said with a smirk.

"That's not even why I came over here . . . "

"Spirituality is a private thing. Very private, Clipper," A. C. interrupted.

Clipper retorted, angry now, "If spirituality is such a private thing, then why do get your thrills from threatening our prayer group?"

"What threats?" A. C. asked calmly.

"Don't tell me you don't know about it."

"Maybe I do. Maybe I don't. You've probably had lots of threats," A. C. said, finally turning to look at Clipper. "Look, I'm not responsible for everything bad that happens to you. You need to understand that. I'm not the one who came to you. *You* came to *me*. I'm not the one making the threats on the meeting you're gonna have at the flagpole. But I am warning you. Be careful, Clipper. I know these people."

"Who?"

"These *kinds* of people, I mean. Take what you hear as promises, not threats."

Eli finally saw Autumn at the end of the school day as she was leaving the library. She camped out there during every free moment preparing for the first regional debate of the year. He caught up with her as she was leaving and tapped her on the shoulder.

"You were incredible!"

"What are you talking about?" Autumn asked, surprised to see the handsome athlete.

"The town-hall meeting," Eli replied.

"You saw it?" Autumn was surprised. Eli didn't exactly strike her as the public television type.

"I was thinking about you while I was channel surfing last night. So when I saw you, I thought I was hallucinating. The woman of my dreams was on PBS."

"You really *are* demented, aren't you?" Autumn was flattered, but didn't know how to react.

"Why didn't you tell me you were gonna be on TV? We really need to work on our communication skills," Eli said earnestly.

"It wasn't something I planned to do. I just felt my hand go up and the next thing I knew they stuck a mike in my face."

"That old guy, Senator What's-his-name . . . "

"Lindsay."

"Right. He looked pretty flustered. You really got to him."

"I'm a trained professional," Autumn replied in a pseudo-serious tone.

They walked together out of the foyer of the main building and into a stiff September breeze, neither of them speaking. Autumn dreaded where talking with Eli might lead. *He might use the "d" word,* she thought to herself, *date.*

She had always hidden behind her father, her schedule, or the debate team. Every now and then, when her schedule settled, she wondered what having a boyfriend would be like, but she saw the emotional upheaval her friends experienced when relationships faded, and she determined in her heart that wouldn't happen to her. She also realized that Eli's interest in sports and her interest in debating and politics created a wide sociological chasm between them.

"So, what do you have planned for Friday night?" Eli asked her.

"Friday night? What did you have in mind?" Autumn asked, looking away as her mind searched for excuses.

"I've got a game Friday night, and I thought you might want to come watch," Eli said hesitantly.

Autumn was relieved at the fairly innocent suggestion, but then he continued.

"Then I thought maybe we could . . . "

"Eli," Autumn interrupted, "I hope you understand. Right now I'm just so busy . . . "

"I understand," Eli said with a forced smile.

"No wait. Let me finish. I'm just—" Autumn paused, for once at a loss for words. *Communication is my forte. Just talk!* she thought to herself. "I just need you to be patient with me." *What am I saying? Patient for what?* "Can we take things slowly and just be friends for now?"

"That's all I want," Eli said. "Believe me, I'm not on my knees with a ring in my pocket."

"OK, OK, I believe you," Autumn said, embarrassed.

"Look, I know you're not really into football," Eli said. "Why don't I just meet you Sunday morning at church. Since your dad's the preacher, he'll be in a perfect place to oversee my behavior."

Autumn smiled, "It's a date—well, you know what I mean."

"So, how was school?" Clipper's mom asked as he walked in.

"Oh, you know, Mom. Same old stuff . . . drug smuggling, gang wars, fire drills, sword fighting, Salisbury steak . . . " Clipper said casually as he plopped on the couch and flipped the TV to ESPN2.

His mom ignored the reply. "Guess what I found in our mailbox today. A letter from Louisville addressed to a Mr. Clipper Hayes. Do you know who that is?"

Clipper popped up like he'd been hit by a bolt of lightning and hurried to retrieve the letter. *Finally, a letter from Jenny,* he thought.

"So, are you going to read it to me?" his mother asked with a wink.

"Funny," he said dryly, not looking up from the envelope. He walked straight to his room and carefully opened the letter with his pocketknife.

He had anxiously waited to hear from Jenny, who was sent to Louisville by her parents to have her baby. He'd never had strong feelings for any girl like he did for Jenny. They had dated just a few times before she found out that she was going to have a baby from a past relationship. Most guys would have blown her off after finding out. But Clipper never felt that way. He unfolded the paper decorated with flowers around the border.

*Dear Clipper,*

*I'm sorry I haven't written you. You've been so sweet to me. I'm still so ashamed about the mess I've gotten myself into.*

*Every time I read your letters I'm reminded how lucky I am to have a friend like you. I don't know why you still care for me. I wasn't up front with you. I didn't let you know what was really going on with me. I was so ashamed. I knew from the first time we talked that you were spiritually strong. I dated you because I wanted a retreat from all the guys who were only after one thing.*

*We've been through all of this before, but I wanted to tell you again that I admire you. I really do. After you heard I was pregnant, you could have completely written me off. But you didn't. In fact, you kept me from doing something that I would have regretted the rest of my life. I'll always be grateful to you for that, Clip.*

*I feel so isolated here in Louisville. My parents call me every week, but the conversation is so surface. I know I've disappointed them. I don't think they'll ever get over the shame they feel because of me.*

*I have gained something from this experience. I've learned to pray. Some days prayer is the only thing that keeps me sane.*

*Some nights I stay awake and replay all the mistakes I made over the past few months. Why did I get drunk that night? Why did I stick around at that party when Tim came back from college? If only I had just left that night, I wouldn't be here. If only . . .*

*So many regrets. So much hurt. Some nights I dream that I'm back in Indy, that I'm there with you. But then I wake up, and I remember that I'm here and pregnant and alone.*

*I really haven't been feeling well, and I know that's making things seem a hundred times worse. I know I've never been pregnant before, but something just doesn't feel right. I'm scared, and I miss you. I feel like you're the only family I have anymore. I love you, and I hope to see you soon.*

> *Love,*
> *Jenny*

Clipper read the note again and wondered how he could last another day without burning the interstate to Louisville.

Later that evening, Clipper sat his parents down and calmly said, "I need to go."

"Is she all right?" Mrs. Hayes asked.

"That's just it. I don't know. She says she doesn't feel well, and she feels like I'm the only family she has."

"What about her parents?"

Clipper shook his head and said cynically, "Her parents don't give a rip."

Clipper's dad said, "Now, you don't know that." He rubbed his chin, then added, "It's not our place to barge into this."

"Maybe not, Dad, but I need to go see her. That wouldn't be barging in," Clipper persisted.

The three of them were silent as they pondered the situation. Finally Mr. Hayes spoke, "I think he should go. It would do Jenny good. And I suspect Clip isn't going to give us a moment's peace otherwise."

"Can I go tonight?" Clipper asked excitedly.

"Saturday," Mrs. Hayes countered.

"Saturday?" Clipper said, his face falling with disappointment.

"Well . . . OK, Friday," his mother conceded.

"Morning?" asked Clipper, still bargaining for as much time as possible.

"After school. As long as someone goes with you," Mr. Hayes said in a tone that left no room for argument.

Autumn was hurriedly gathering her books and her purse for school when her father, Rev. Sanders, knocked on her bedroom door. "Autumn? Telephone."

"Got it, Dad," she said, reaching for the phone on her desk. "Hello?"

"Good morning, Autumn."

Autumn furrowed her brow. "Yes?" she said hesitantly, not recognizing the voice.

"This is Jim Cleary, candidate for state senate."

Autumn smiled and rolled her eyes.

"Yeah, right. Did Clipper put you up to this?" Autumn said in total disbelief.

"I'm afraid not. Really, this is Jim. Jim Cleary. I'm the Republican candidate that you helped get a real jump with your statistical wizardry the other night."

"Wait. Hold it. Tell me again. You're—"

"James C. Cleary," he said distinctly. "I'm running for senate. You *do* remember the town-hall meeting don't you?"

"Yes."

"I want to invite you to a meeting tonight," Cleary said casually.

"A meeting. Like another debate?" Autumn asked, guessing that Cleary was doing a phone blitz for his campaign.

Cleary laughed. "No, not another debate. I'm just taking my campaign staff out to eat tonight, and I wanted to see if you could join us. Judging from what I heard Monday night, I think you have a tremendous mind for politics. I have been looking for an edge ever since I began my campaign. Lindsay has been in the senate for years, and if I'm going to win, I need to demonstrate that I have new ideas. Do you think you could help?"

Autumn's mind raced. She couldn't figure out what the handsome politician could want with her, although she was pretty sure that Cleary wasn't asking her to stuff envelopes or deliver door hangers.

Cleary had paused and waited for a response. Finally he said, "Hello? Autumn?"

"I'm sorry," Autumn finally responded, "I'm kind of at a loss here. I don't understand. Why do you want me to come to this dinner? If it's like a fund-raising thing then—"

Cleary laughed again, "No, it's not a fund-raising deal. I remember enough of my teenage years to know that high school students don't have very deep pockets."

"So then . . . " Autumn said with a lilt in her voice, waiting for him to fill in the blank.

"Well, I wasn't going to ask you this so soon. But I guess I'll go ahead and trust my instinct. I mean, my back's against the wall. I wanted to see if you'd come on my staff as a consultant."

"A consultant? Me?" Autumn said dumbfounded.

"Yes, you. I couldn't get you out of my mind after the debate. You remember when you said you couldn't vote but that you hoped citizens would look out for your future?"

Embarrassed that he'd paid that much attention to what she'd said that evening, Autumn blushed. "Yes, I meant what I said."

"That was an incredible statement. I kept trying to recall where I'd seen you before, and I remembered seeing you in the paper. You'd won some award in debate or something. Then it all started coming together."

"What came together?" Autumn interjected.

"If I'm going to have any chance at defeating Lindsay, I'm going to need to appeal to a younger demographic. I think choosing Autumn Sanders to be on my staff would appeal to lots of people who otherwise wouldn't give me any serious consideration."

"So I'd be your poster girl for the youth issues?"

Cleary backtracked quickly. "No. That's not what I'm saying. Like I said, I think you are tremendously articulate and have an incredible mind. I want you to help me shape this campaign. You'll be a real part of the team. You won't be just the token student on staff. This is an incredible opportunity—for both of us."

Autumn was rendered speechless by the proposal.

After a moment, Cleary asked, "So, can I have my administrative assistant call you with directions and so forth?"

Trying to hide her shock and sound as mature and professional as possible, Autumn said, "Yes, I look forward to it, really. Thanks so much for asking."

"My pleasure. See you tonight."

A. C. couldn't recall when his anger toward the church and God began. It seemed he had always felt it. Perhaps because he never really had a family. That might have been why the anger erupted in his life. He had lived in ten different homes in the past five years, shifting back and forth between his biological family and foster homes.

In the midst of all the turmoil and anger he felt, he found himself surrounded by people who shared an anger toward God and the suburban society as a whole. He adopted their ideas and regarded Christians as idealistic and fake, not really caring for those outside of their own picket-fenced neighborhoods. Then he encountered Clipper, a guy who wouldn't be shoved away. Clipper had edged his way into A. C.'s life, and A. C. had moved from loathing to a quiet respect for him.

But A. C. knew that he had to distance himself from Clipper if he wanted to do the things he and his friends dared themselves to do.

They wanted to make a statement. A loud exclamation point behind their belief that prayer should remain in the churches and that if these Jesus freaks brought prayer into the school, they would bring destruction into the churches. Their plan was simply to bomb a church building if students at Summit carried out "See You at the Pole."

"You need to stay away from Clipper," the guy nicknamed van Gogh insisted. "Your relationship with this guy isn't good. You're starting to scare me."

"Why?"

"I can tell you're thinkin' too much about this. Don't go soft on us," van Gogh said.

"I have been thinking, but not because of him."

"Well, then stop thinking. This is our moment of destiny!" van Gogh said fervently. "Too much planning has gone into this. Point of no return, man. We've got to let them know who runs the show around here. You're gonna help us turn this thing. If they pray next Wednesday, then a church is going down."

Kandi fell onto the library couch after her dance class. She had fifteen minutes of solitude and relaxation after a host of pliés, spins, stretches, and leaps before she entered into the torture chamber of chemistry. She picked up a *Time* magazine and pretended to read. Her eyes wouldn't even focus on the pictures, but this charade was mandatory in order to appease the librarians.

After a few moments, a student she had never met handed her a note. Kandi looked at the girl strangely. The girl just shrugged her shoulders and walked away. Kandi smiled, amused by her awkward manner and quick, silent exit.

Kandi opened the hand-written note and read.

*Your presence is requested at stack fifteen on the second tier.*

Kandi hesitated. After all the things she had been through at Summit, she found anonymous invitations a little unsettling. Finally she stood up and whispered cynically to herself, "What now?"

She climbed the stairs slowly and navigated to stack fifteen. She leaned around the corner and peered down the aisle. No one. *Must be Justin or Clipper,* she thought to herself, shaking her head. She leaned against the shelf for just a moment before someone whispered, "Hey."

Kandi almost jumped out of her skin as she spun around and looked through the books. There she saw Eli's blond-haired friend, Zack Galloway, who had doused her the day before.

Kandi's glare could have burned a hole through an encyclopedia. "Yes?"

"Hi! I'm Zack. The guy who misfired with the water balloon."

Kandi crossed her arms and said with a cold tone, "How could I forget? I suppose this is you," she said as she held the note up to his eye level. "Do you always impose on people like this?"

"Impose?" Zack questioned.

"I mean, first, it's the adolescent prank and now it's the mystery note. I was relaxed, comfortable and you—"

"Sorry," Zack said sincerely. "I couldn't exactly get down on my hands and knees and apologize with our ninety-year-old librarian breathing down my back. She'd condemn me to library purgatory or worse."

"OK. You've apologized. Apology accepted," Kandi said with a polite yet forced smile.

Zack just stood there and nodded with a proud smile on his face. His smile disarmed her. She could only see his eyes and nose through the rows of books, but she could see in his bright blue eyes that he was smiling.

"So that's it?" Kandi said hesitantly.

"I thought maybe we could get to know each other a little better."

"What?" Kandi was surprised that he would even ask.

"I know this is absolutely nuts. I mean I drop a balloon on you, and then I ask you out," Zack said.

"Ask me out?" Kandi repeated.

"No," he said quickly, backing away a little. "I just—what I meant was that—OK, can I start over?"

"Uh, nope," Kandi said as she shook her head and walked away.

"So you're just gonna leave."

"Right," Kandi replied.

"That's impolite," Zack said, playfully following her movement down the aisle.

"Impolite?!" Kandi exclaimed, amazed at his forwardness. "I think impolite is when you douse someone with cold water before school starts so that she gets an unexcused absence and has to do double homework in first period. Now that's what I call impolite," Kandi finished.

"Sorry. I am so sorry. What else can I do? I just hate that I did that," Zack said as they met at the end of the stack.

Kandi got her first full look at the water-balloon terrorist. Something about seeing him, standing close to him, softened her.

He continued, pleading for her attention, "I didn't do it intentionally, and ever since that time, I just had to find you to tell you that I wanted—I want to make it up to you."

"So you want to make it up to me," Kandi said, not sure what she would say if he asked her out. Certainly Eli would have told him that she was in a dating relationship. Surely he would have said something about Justin. "Really, you don't have to do anything. I accepted your apology," Kandi said quickly.

"You did? Didn't sound like it," Zack said.

"It didn't?" Kandi said, amazed by his persistence.

"It sounded like, 'OK, fine. Get out of my face.' And that's just not good enough for me," Zack said as he admired her appearance.

Kandi backed up, feeling uncomfortable now about the lack of distance between them. "Not good enough for you?"

"No. Not good enough." He stepped up each time she stepped back.

"What did you want me to say?" Kandi said as her mind raced, wondering why she hadn't walked away from the conversation.

"It's not what I wanted you to say. It's what I wanted you to feel," Zack said.

"I've gotta go. This has been uh—thanks for the apology. Trust me. I accept it. And I mean it. OK?"

"Still not good enough," Zack said as she walked away. "We need to get to know each other."

"Yeah. Right."

Kandi turned back around and said in a voice too loud for the library, "You aren't one of those stalkers that end up on 'Court TV' or 'Judge Judy' are you?"

"Funny girl . . . You need to get to know me," Zack said.

"At this point, it looks like I don't have a choice," Kandi said as she walked down the stairs and hurried out of the library.

For the rest of the day, she couldn't get his name or his face out of her mind. It became somewhat irksome to her because she really didn't want to fall for a guy with a ponytail and a diamond earring. She didn't want to put up with his crazy antics. Certainly the water balloon deal was a fluke. But she did feel amused, and even flattered by his awkward disjointed attempt at flirting. "I have a feeling I haven't heard the last from this guy," she said to herself with dread and hope combined.

Justin and Clipper walked quickly to Justin's car after school, hoping to beat the oncoming storm clouds that filled the western sky.

"So you'll go to Louisville with me?" Clipper asked.

"If I can get off work," Justin replied.

"Because if you can't go, I can't go," Clipper said with a heaviness in his voice.

"Mom and Dad's rules?" Justin said as he opened the door and flipped the automatic door lock for Clipper.

"Mom and Dad," Clipper said as he rolled his eyes.

"I don't know why they trust me," Justin said.

"Beats me," Clipper said.

"So what are you expecting when you get there?" Justin asked curiously.

"I don't know what to expect. My relationship with Jenny has always been strange. The last time we talked, I said I wanted to be a friend, a brother. She agreed." He frowned, then continued, "She agreed as soon as I said it. She didn't even think about it. She just said, 'I think that you're right.' And I really thought that was the best scenario for everyone. I felt great about it then, but twenty-four hours later, after she'd left for Louisville and life returned to normal, those feelings of wanting more came back with a vengeance."

"And that's when the Guinness world record of un-answered letters began," Justin added.

"Right. I wrote a letter, and she never wrote me back. I waited a week, and then I wrote another and another and another. Then she writes me and says she wants to see me," Clipper continued.

"About what?" Justin asked suspiciously.

"Not a clue," Clipper said. "If only I had a talent for relating to girls like you have. Life would be a whole lot easier."

"I'd have to disagree big time on that one, Clip," Justin said as dots of water appeared on his windshield from an oncoming afternoon shower. "Figuring Kandi out is an art I haven't acquired either."

"Things OK?"

"Hardly," Justin replied.

"What is it?"

"Just stuff. We seem to be in a rut. We go out and do things all the time, but I don't think we're connecting. Lately I feel more like a big brother than her boyfriend," Justin said bluntly.

Clipper just stared at him in disbelief. "Are you joking?"

"Nope."

As they drove down the road, Clipper and Justin were awk-wardly silent for a few moments. Finally Clipper asked, "What did you make of the E-mail that Luke sent to everyone?"

"I knew there were some threats but nothing more than pranks in my opinion," Justin said casually, without real concern. "Anything I don't know about?"

"Not really," Clipper said.

"What?"

"Nothing. Nothing at all." Clipper tried to keep his tone firm.

"Did your bud, A. C., tell you anything?" Justin asked.

"He just said that he wasn't a part of it."

"Course not," Justin said sarcastically.

"I believe him," Clipper shot back defensively.

"Why?" Justin shot back. "It smells like something his crowd would do if you ask me."

"It may be his crowd, but it ain't him," Clipper said, distancing himself from Justin's attitude. "He just thought we should take the threats seriously."

"We can't take threats seriously when they haven't given us any idea what they are threatening us with," Justin said.

"Agreed. But I'd bet they'll give us more details soon."

"Doesn't matter to me. We aren't going to cancel 'See You at the Pole' at Summit just because A. C. thinks it wouldn't be a good idea," Justin replied. As they drove down Flanders Avenue, Justin slowed down. "Clipper, grab that book on the floorboard. I need to return it. It's overdue."

Clipper reached down and grabbed the fifty-year-old Civil War textbook. He flipped through the archaic pages of plain text with a few line illustrations and charts. The musty aroma tickled Clipper's nose, which exploded with a tumultuous sneeze. "I officially declare this book condemned. You know they've written newer books on the subject."

"I know. But I figure the Civil War hasn't changed much in the past century. Plus it was the only book I could find. I think the teachers across Indy plot against us. They all scream for research papers on the same subject simultaneously."

"I know. It's like some kind of scholastic harmonic convergence. A conspiracy. Definitely a conspiracy."

Clipper saw a note sticking out of the back of the book. He pulled out the note, which was on plain white paper folded a few times. Justin's name was typed on the outside. Clipper, impressed by the businesslike appearance of the note, raised his eyebrows and said, "So whose got a crush on you? The president's daughter?"

"What?" Justin said.

"This note; it's so professional, so clean," Clipper said as his eyes darted over to Justin in curiosity.

"I didn't have anything in there," Justin said, trying to look at the note and watch the road.

"Yes, you did," said Clipper.

"Did not."

"Then where'd it come from?" Clipper flashed the note so that Justin could see his name on the outside fold.

Justin grabbed the note as he drove. His eyes cut back and forth from the road to the note. At a stoplight, he unfolded it and read silently. Clipper waited for him to smile, feeling certain it was probably an infatuated freshman. Clipper had grown accustomed to seeing girls fall for Justin and, in a lot of ways, Clipper felt relieved he didn't have to deal with that kind of pressure. But Justin wasn't smiling as he read the note. His demeanor was solemn.

"What is it?" Clipper asked.

"Nothing," Justin said as he wadded the note.

"Yeah, right. What is it?" Clipper asked again.

"It's not important," Justin replied as he looked straight ahead, waiting for the light to change.

"I don't care if it's not important. I want to know what it is. You know me. Gotta know. Just have to know. You wouldn't have seen the note if I hadn't given it to you."

Justin tried to laugh casually, obviously downplaying whatever he had read. "Just our little twisted friends. Guess they've decided to expand the game."

He tossed the note over to Clipper. "They really don't want prayer in school."

Clipper read the note, which held the newest, most specific threat:

*Don't pray at Summit or a church will be destroyed.*
                                                      *—van Gogh*

Autumn walked briskly through the halls of the school the next morning. She had never felt such exhilaration as she did after her meeting with James Cleary the night before. She felt a new kind of confidence. The experience transported her from the normality of high school into a new and exciting world. Cleary had treated her with as much respect as he had his senior advisor. And she wasn't even nervous. Ideas and words flowed effortlessly from her as they brainstormed youth issues, teen pregnancy, scholarship policy, and victims' rights

Cleary never took his eyes off her when she talked. He smiled and shook his head in disbelief at her knowledge of political issues and policy. Even when others were speaking, she caught him staring at her. *What was he thinking?* Autumn asked herself.

She replayed the best moment of the evening. Cleary had publicly asked her to join his campaign staff. She could still hear the applause when she accepted. She could still feel the surprise as he suddenly reached out to embrace her. The entire experience left her unable to sleep until the early morning hours.

Despite the lack of sleep, though, Autumn felt energized and passionate about her future. She couldn't wait to tell Sandy Moore, her debate coach. Mrs. Moore was more than a coach. Since coming to Summit, Sandy had been a mentor, friend, and trusted confidant. Autumn moved even faster as she saw her teacher in the classroom.

"He asked me to join his campaign staff," Autumn exclaimed without even greeting the teacher.

"He who?" Mrs. Moore said, in disbelief.

"James Cleary wants me on his staff!" Autumn said, almost bursting with excitement.

"That's incredible! Cleary? James Cleary. I don't understand. How did he find you?" Mrs. Moore said, still astonished by Autumn's news.

Autumn shrugged her shoulders. "He's a politician and a lawyer. That's how he makes his living," she said, giggling.

Mrs. Moore's sudden tight embrace almost took her breath away. To her, Autumn had done the equivalent of winning a national speech tournament. When they broke from their embrace, Autumn was surprised to see tears in her teacher's eyes.

"I'm sorry," Mrs. Moore said and hugged her again. "I'm just so happy for you. I've known ever since I met you that you were special. It's like this voice inside of me said you were going to do extraordinary things. I'm so proud." She reached for a tissue on her desk, "And now look at me, a blubbering idiot," she said as she laughed and cried at the same time.

Autumn's chin quivered slightly as she fought back emotions.

"I've known all along that if I invested time with you I'd be thankful for years to come. You have such a great and important future ahead of you."

"That's why I wanted to tell you this before I even told my parents," Autumn said. "To tell you the truth, I wasn't sure if you'd be all that excited about this, with all the research for the debates we have scheduled."

"Autumn," Mrs. Moore said in a motherly tone, "you have been given a chance to practice what you've learned. Debate is training camp. They just called you up to the big league, and you have the talent to do whatever you want. This is the starting place. You *need* to do this. Even if it means you need to pull out of the debate team for a while."

Kandi went to the school library that morning and searched halfheartedly through shelves for a reference that might help her complete her project on the War of 1812. She knew she shouldn't have procrastinated this long, but she didn't have the energy for it. As her eyes scanned the books, she thought of the last time she stood there, remembering Zack's avante garde personality that had irked and secretly delighted her. She wondered why she felt that way about him. There was something about him that made her smile, and she didn't have any idea why. *Here's a guy who drenched me when we first met, lured me up the stairs with an anonymous letter so he could apologize and come on to me, simultaneously,* she thought to herself. *What's there to be delighted about?*

She tried to put these thoughts out of her mind and return to 1812. A title caught her eye: *The Forgotten Conflict: 1812.* It had to be four inches thick. *There's no way I'm lugging that thing home,* Kandi thought to herself. Still, she pulled the volume from the shelf for a closer look. As she did, she flinched as Zack's face filled the empty space where the book had been.

"You're doing it again!" Kandi said in a loud whisper.

"What?" Zack asked innocently.

"Yeah, right. Like you don't know what I'm talking about. I just want you to stop it. Understand? Stop following me. Wasn't it enough that I had to get bombed by a water balloon from the third floor and then coerced into meeting you yesterday? And now you show up behind my library book! Don't think that I don't get you, Zack. I do! You are stalking me! And if you keep it up, I *will* report it. So don't give me your innocent *what?*"

Kandi's anger turned into embarrassment as another face appeared in the hole between the books. It was Mrs. Gustovson, Zack's history teacher. "I'm afraid that there's been a misunderstanding. I brought Zack up here. He asked me to show him where the Civil War reference books were. I don't think he's stalking you."

Kandi's jaw dropped. She could only walk away embarrassed and speechless. She didn't know where to go. She had work to do in the library, but no matter how urgent the work seemed to be a few minutes ago, she certainly couldn't stay now. She walked out into the corridor toward the commons area. There she met up with Autumn, whose day was clearly off to a better start.

"Hey girl!" Autumn called out to her amid the noise of the usual between-bell traffic. "You won't believe this, but I am having the greatest week of my life!"

"Wish I could say the same," Kandi said honestly.

"You remember me telling you about James Cleary?"

"The senator?"

"Not yet, but I've got a hunch he will be in a couple of months," Autumn said.

Kandi couldn't help noticing the euphoria that seemed to exude from Autumn. She had a girlish carefree countenance that Kandi had never seen before.

"He called me," Autumn said with glee.

"This Cleary guy called you?"

"He called me."

"So, did he ask you out?" Kandi said half joking.

"Funny, Kandi. He asked me to be on his campaign staff," Autumn said as she squeezed Kandi's arm.

Kandi could gage Autumn's enthusiasm by the tightness of the grip on her bicep.

"That's great," Kandi said as she hugged Autumn. "So what does a staff member do?"

"I'm trying to figure that part out," Autumn said, still wide-eyed. "But can you believe he called me?"

"After the town meeting the other night? I can believe it. Justin said you blew everybody out of the water, especially the older candidate. I saw Cleary on the news the other night. Wow, what a guy! He's so tall . . . big brown eyes . . . Are you sure this is all political?" Kandi asked as she smiled mischievously.

"I have to admit, he's pretty cute," Autumn said hesitantly.

Kandi was surprised by Autumn's reply. She expected to get a lecture from her on several levels. Kandi loved jabbing Autumn's prudent, no-nonsense lifestyle. Her admission of being attracted to this man threw Kandi for a loop. Kandi leaned in an inch closer. "What?"

"I just mean he's a really nice guy. He's brilliant and he's—"

"Did I just hear you say you thought he was cute?" Kandi asked again, smiling as she did.

"I don't think I meant it like you heard it," Autumn said, trying desperately to backtrack.

"'I have to admit, he's pretty cute.' Those were your exact words," Kandi said, still smiling as Autumn began to walk backwards and bumped into a student.

"OK! OK! I think he's cute. He's a guy in his thirties, who is single, who is politically on target, and I happen to think he's cute. So what? I think Denzel Washington is cute. That doesn't mean I'm going to search the net for his E-mail address so I can ask him out on a date."

"Yeah. Right," Kandi replied.

"You don't buy the analogy, do you?" Autumn stated. "Do you really think that I would—"

Much to Autumn's frustration, Kandi kept on smiling.

As her fifth period class discussed the psychological aspects of *Hamlet,* Autumn's attention was divided between Shakespeare and Cleary. She thought about the brief conversation with Kandi, dismissing Kandi's playful conclusions. Still, the more she thought about the words that had fallen so easily from her lips, the more she began to wonder if she really did have feelings beyond admiration for Jim Cleary.

Throughout the day her mind compulsively returned to the few conversations with Cleary. She recalled the dialogue, the nuances, the clever way he crafted sentences. She recalled how he seemed to listen, even during the staff meeting the night before. When she spoke, he seemed to block out everyone in the room and concentrate on every word she said. This kind of attention was a rare commodity in her world, where debaters listened with one ear and furiously wrote notes and searched for index cards with the other.

Autumn felt the vibration of her pager on her hip and reached down to check the number. She didn't recognize it. *Wrong number,* she thought to herself until she remembered giving the number to Mr. Cleary. Her heart raced a little faster as she stared at the pager and then quickly, discreetly attached it to her waist again. She counted the seconds for the bell to ring. She had to find a phone and felt almost embarrassed by her status as a mere high school student at the mercy of teachers and bells.

"Hello?" The voice on the other end of the line said.

Autumn felt sure that it was Jim Cleary but didn't want to assume. "I received a page a few minutes ago from this number and . . . "

"Autumn. How are you? Look, I'm really sorry to disturb you. I didn't think you'd get the page until school was out," Cleary's voice said amicably.

"I sort of accidentally left it on. What can I do for you, Mr. Cleary?" she said casually.

"Autumn, Autumn, Autumn, when are you gonna stop calling me Mr. Cleary. You make me feel like an old man."

"Sorry. Habit, I guess." Autumn said smiling, looking around at the bustling mass of students who passed within inches of her. She was embarrassed by her surroundings as she talked to him.

"When will you be free? I'd like you to come by and help us with an item we want to add to the brochure on youth issues and education. Larry gave me some stats on school dropouts, but just between you and me, I trust your research more. Could you come by tonight?"

Autumn uncharacteristically ignored checking her day planner and answered immediately, "Sure. What time?"

"How does six sound to you?" Cleary replied.

"Six is great," Autumn said enthusiastically.

"Don't eat. I'm treating everybody to Chinese take-out. We've got a lot to do and the more caffeine and MSG, the better," he finished, laughing.

James Cleary had practiced law in Indianapolis for three years, since moving to Indy from Duluth, Minnesota. The press treated him like the golden boy of Indianapolis after he won a high-profile suit against a local industry with an unlawful policy that harmed lower-level employees. Some predicted he could be the governor of the state within the next few years. Autumn had heard it all and couldn't believe that in a week's time she would be helping him on his first major campaign.

Autumn pulled up to Jim Cleary's office complex just before six. The nearly vacant parking lot surprised her. She wondered if she had misunderstood his invitation. *Didn't he say the entire staff would be here?* she asked herself.

She walked to the door and opened it. A small lamp at the receptionist's desk was the only source of light in the outer office.

"Hello?" Autumn said timidly.

"Come in," a voice from inside the office called out.

Autumn walked over and pushed the door open wider.

"Hey, Autumn. Glad you could make it!" Cleary said.

"Did I mistake the time? I thought the staff was going to be working late," Autumn said, somewhat confused. The empty office was disturbed only by the quiet hum of the desktop computers and the whisper of the light jazz from the radio.

"I just let them go early. We had some things come up— issues I knew had to be dealt with tomorrow. So, I told them to go home, get some rest, and come back fresh in the morning. When you're working on something as consuming as this race, you just have to let the team breathe. I hope you don't mind—"

"Me? Of course not. What's there to mind?" Autumn said, embarrassed. "We can meet later. Are you heading out now?"

"I'm in it for the long haul, I'm afraid, and I was kind of hoping you could do that research tonight as well. If you're hungry, I could still order out."

Her mind raced, sizing up the situation and wondering to herself why she felt a twinge of discomfort. After a second of thought, she blurted out, "Of course I can stay. And I'm not really hungry. I mean, you just wanted me to verify Larry's stuff, and I certainly can do that by myself before I go home."

"Great. I've fired up Netscape on the computer, and I bookmarked some of the sites he used to get the information. Give me your opinion about whether you think these sites look legitimate. I'm a bit suspicious of the stuff we get off the Internet."

"I'll take a look at it, and then make some calls if I need to. No prob," she said smiling.

"Super. I'm glad you're here tonight. I knew they needed a break, but I wasn't looking forward to plowing ahead alone, if you know what I mean."

"I guess. I'm kind of a loner when it comes to this kind of thing. Research is a lonely job but somebody's got to do it," Autumn said awkwardly and wondered when she had decided to become the queen of clichés.

Being there alone with Cleary was unnerving, especially after hearing Kandi's innuendoes earlier in the day. Autumn realized this was one of the few times she had worked alone with a man. When she thought of her growing attraction to him, she felt nervous and uneasy, but she felt she couldn't leave. What would that say to him if she opted out? To her, it would seem to say, *I'm a child, and I am out of my league.* She didn't want to make that between-the-lines statement, so she stayed. *But Dad would freak if he knew the situation,* she thought to herself.

For an hour they worked without talking. Autumn immersed herself in the task, trying to divert her mind from the unusual situation. She could hear him on the phone in his office. Every now and then her mind drifted as she listened to him. His voice warmed her. His laughter made her smile.

Autumn looked up at the clock. It was 7:30. She had told her parents she'd be back late, which was nothing new to them. They had grown accustomed to her work habits, and they trusted her completely. As she shut down the computer and stood to stretch, she heard Jim get up from his desk. He leaned against the frame of his office door, smiling.

"Are you going to let me in on it?" Autumn said, smiling shyly.

"In on what?"

"On why you're smiling," Autumn replied.

"Just looking at you," Jim Cleary said.

Autumn was caught off guard by the comment and felt herself blushing. Was she paranoid, or was he making a pass at her? She quickly dismissed the idea as ridiculous and changed the subject. "I think all of these sources are correct, with the exception of the school lunch figures. That was a typo, I suppose, because the source he identified declared a $50,000 increase."

Cleary didn't even acknowledge her attempt to deflect his remark. "You have so much to look forward to. You're so young. So smart. I look at you, and I'm jealous."

Autumn laughed nervously, "Jealous? Believe me, you have nothing to be jealous about. You've got everything you need. Your future's great. You have a clean record. People love you around here. You'll beat Lindsay by 15 percent or more. And you'd rather be a sixteen-year-old female high school student who still has a curfew? You've been working too hard. You're hallucinating," she said playfully.

"Hallucinating?" Cleary said, smiling.

"You got it, Cleary."

"I truly hate it when you call me that," he said as he walked over beside her.

Her heart pounded. Surely he could see her hands trembling slightly. She stood there not knowing what he was doing and not sure she had the willpower to resist him if he embraced her.

He reached out and put his hand on her shoulder. His warm hand resting on her, his eyes looking squarely into hers, seemed more of a comfort than a threat, but she knew she had

to retreat. No matter how incredible and yet seemingly innocent this moment was, she knew it was inappropriate.

"Jim, I've really got to go," Autumn said, matter-of-factly. The
sudden change caused Clearly to flinch slightly, as if waking
from a peaceful dream.

"Really?" he asked.

"Really," she said firmly.

"I guess it *is* getting kind of late," Cleary said as he looked
at his watch.

"Right," Autumn said. She quickly grabbed her purse and
book bag.

"Sorry I kept you out so late," he apologized.

"No problem. I just have to go. I have some things I need
to finish for school."

"You can work here if you'd like," Cleary offered.

"No. I really need to head home. Thanks, though," Autumn
said. The moment became increasingly businesslike and awkward. "I appreciate it. Maybe some other time, but I've got to
go. I really do." She opened the door.

"Is everything—"

"Everything's fine, Mr. Cleary . . . I mean Jim. I'll just . . . well
give me a call . . . I mean when you need me to help you or . . ."

"Autumn," Cleary interrupted, "you're a member of the
team. You're not a hired temp. I'll see you tomorrow. Drop by
after school. We're going to press with the flyer by the end of
the week," Cleary said.

"Right. I'll see you tomorrow afternoon then."

A. C. lived with his grandmother. As he walked up the porch steps of her house, he saw, for the first time in three months, his father, casually sitting on the porch swing. A. C. didn't even try to keep track of the time lapses anymore. His mom and dad had both abandoned him shortly after his birth. His mom left without a trace, while his father popped in and out of A. C.'s life at odd and inconvenient times.

The younger man stared at his father, hoping the man would see the complete disgust A. C. felt for him. His gaze swept over his father's disheveled appearance—dirty jeans, a rumpled Grateful Dead T-shirt, and a cigarette hanging loosely from his mouth. He didn't even bother to take it out when he spoke.

"Hey kid, you doing OK?" Ric asked.

"What's it to you?" A. C. said, offering no sign of interest as he unlocked the front door.

"It's been a while," Ric said as he stood.

"Not nearly long enough," A. C. said. "I don't think you came just to see me. What do you want?"

"Maybe I did come to see you," Ric said defensively.

"OK. You've seen me," A. C. said, and began to shut the door.

Ric put his forearm out to block it from closing. "Hang on a sec. What do you think you're doing? Where's your grandma?"

"She's working," A. C. said, growing impatient with the conversation. "Would you please get out of my face?"

"I'm coming in," his dad said.

"No you aren't," A. C. said. Ric grabbed a handful of A. C.'s shirt collar and pushed him out of the entrance. He strutted inside, tossing his cigarette butt into the sink filled with dirty dishes. "I need a loan," he grunted. "Where's she keeping the stash? She always had a stash somewhere."

"It wouldn't be a loan and you know it. If she gave you any money, she'd never see it again." A. C. spoke through clenched teeth.

"Shut up!" Ric screamed. "I need some money. Now!"

A. C. couldn't take it anymore. He charged his father, tackling him around the midsection. They both landed on the floor. A. C. landed a punch on his dad's jaw and blood appeared. Ric grabbed his son's shoulders and rolled over on top of him, answering the blow with a much harder one.

Ric screamed at his son as A. C. braced himself for further blows. "Don't you ever hit me like that again, or I swear I'll slice you into pieces. You hear me? Don't you ever do that again!"

"Get off of me. Leave me alone."

Ric got up and walked into A. C.'s grandmother's bedroom. A. C. could hear his father tearing through all of her drawers, searching relentlessly for anything of value. He heard the sound of her jewelry box being tossed around and the obscenities his father muttered as he looted his own mother's small, yet prized possessions. A. C. felt a sense of utter insignificance and worthlessness as he thought to himself, *This is the man who was responsible for bringing me into the world.*

After a few moments Ric walked back into the living room. A. C. was too angry to even move. He felt so much rage that he thought he might explode from the inside. His forehead throbbed, both from the blow delivered by his father's fist and his rising anger—the seething rage he had carried most of his life. He didn't know what to do with all the anger he had. This was just the latest in a series of abuses. He felt destined, in many ways, to follow in this man's footsteps even though he hated everything about his father.

Ric tossed a pack of cigarettes to A. C. The pack tapped A. C.'s chest, then fell to the floor. "Don't say I didn't get you anything for your birthday last year," Ric said with a villainous smile. "Enjoy."

A. C. said nothing. He stood motionless, afraid of his own rage and what he might do if he moved.

Ric closed the door as he walked out to his motorcycle. A. C. heard the deep rumble of the Harley as Ric punched the gas, and then sped away. A. C. still didn't move. His breathing became shallow and fast. His eyes moistened, and his throat ached until he couldn't hold back the flood of emotions. He fell to the floor and buried his head in his grandmother's worn carpet. He moaned like a wounded animal under the weight of the years of disappointment, addiction, abuse, and nothingness.

Autumn hadn't planned to talk with Kandi about what happened in Cleary's office the night before, but as they drove to school the next morning, the story slowly came out. "It was so . . . weird," Autumn said with a sigh.

"Weird as in what?" Kandi asked.

"I don't know. Just unusual," Autumn said as she drove.

"Every story has a beginning. So you went over to the office to work with the staff and . . . "

"And he was there without the staff," Autumn said.

"So where were they?" Kandi asked.

"He said he let them go home early to get rest. It just seemed so weird. When he asked me to come, he almost sounded panicked with the deadlines they had in front of them. I show up, and no one's there. He said everyone was stressed, and he let them go home. But he wanted me to stick around. Does that seem weird to you at all?"

"Keep talking," Kandi said.

"That's mainly it," Autumn said.

"Mainly?" Kandi asked with a smile. "What did you two do?"

"We worked for a few hours, and then we had this really strange conversation. I don't even remember how it all went. It wasn't so much what he said. It was how he looked at me. He just seemed to be looking at me . . . "

"Like he was about to kiss you or something?" Kandi asked.

"No," Autumn said quickly, with a worried frown on her face. She was quiet, then after a moment slowly said, "Yes."

"Really?" Kandi's eyes widened with surprise.

"Kandi, I don't know about all this. Maybe I'm just seeing things that aren't there." Autumn gripped the steering wheel in frustration.

"So he didn't kiss you," Kandi said, sounding disappointed.

"No!" Autumn shouted.

"Did he touch you?" Kandi asked.

"Yeah, he kind of did. It was innocent. Kind of."

"Kind of?" Kandi asked.

"On the shoulder. He put his hand on my shoulder," Autumn said.

"Was it a hand on the shoulder to help you out the door? Or was it a face-to-face hand-on-the-shoulder move?" Kandi was definitely the more experienced of the two in these matters.

"I don't quite get where you're—"

"Simple. He walks up to you, flatters you, and then stares into your eyes and puts his hand on your shoulder close to your neck. Is that what he did?"

Autumn nodded.

"I think your intuition is on the mark," Kandi concluded. "He's not just giving you an emotional pat on the back, sister."

"I feel guilty," Autumn admitted. "Last time we talked, I told you that I could fall for a guy like that. I've been running this whole thing through my mind, trying to figure out if I led him into this thing," she finished in a rush.

"He led *you* in there," Kandi said assuredly. "He told *you* there would be others working. You're good, Autumn. But not that good. I don't recall you mentioning paging the staff and asking each one to knock off early. Right?"

Autumn laughed and her tension eased. "Thanks, Kandi. I've really been beating myself up over this. I just don't have as much experience with guys as you do. I've been plowing my way through books most of my life. The long-range goal being to get the best education, and then look for the life partner."

"I have to admit, I'm a little jealous of your willpower," Kandi said honestly.

"I don't know. I don't think I had much willpower last night. If he had kissed me, I might not have exactly gone ballistic," Autumn said.

Justin met them in the school parking lot. "Hey Kandi, where were you last night?"

"Last night?"

"I came by your house and you weren't there," Justin said.

"I didn't know you were coming by," Kandi replied.

"I tried calling you all afternoon. Where were you?"

"I had things I needed to do. What are you getting so suspicious about? Don't you think you're being suffocating?" Kandi asked, a critical tone in her voice.

"Suffocating? Just because I wanted to see you last night? You call that suffocating?" Justin demanded.

Autumn interrupted awkwardly, "So, I think I'll just head on in. Have fun kids. Let me know how it turns out." She walked away briskly. She didn't like this. Kandi and Justin, who had seemed like the perfect couple, had been bickering quite a bit lately. The frequent sarcastic exchanges indicated the relationship was losing steam fast.

Later that day Autumn wrote in her journal:

*It was good for me to see Justin and Kandi like that. Not that I want to see them be rude to each other. It sounds weird, but it reminded me why I've always shied away from relationships with guys. The whole dating thing seems incredibly self-destructive. You have two people who really care about each other. They admire each other. The guy opens the door for the girl. They spend hours on the phone just to hear each other breathe. They become so relationship-centered that they lose their own identity. Does it have to be that way? I do believe I'll have a relationship with a guy in the near future. I hope to keep the relationship free of negativity. I know that it will happen to me one day. I want to be in love and have a family. I want to experience that. But not right now . . . I think.*

Clipper and Justin sat in their mass communications class. It was a very popular class, primarily because the teacher was a well-known retired news broadcaster who gave very easy tests. The class would listen to few lectures and lots of Beethoven while Mr. Dumser grabbed a quick nap.

"So, what's the deal with you?" Clipper whispered to Justin over the classical music surrounding them.

Justin shrugged.

"Kandi?"

Justin hesitated, then nodded. "It's just weird. She's acting really weird, and it's driving me crazy. She acts like I'm treating her like my daughter or something."

"What makes you think that?" Clipper asked.

"Those were her exact words," Justin said.

"Ouch. You think she's ready to make a break?" Clipper asked.

"I don't know. I've ceased trying to figure the girl out. I haven't done anything to her. It's just like something out of the clear blue. One moment everything's great: she forgives me for the banquet deal, and we have a great week. Next thing I know, boom. It's like something clicked in her mind and now all of the sudden, I'm acting like her dad."

"She might just be going a little biologically schizoid. It happens," Clipper said.

Justin contorted his brow and repeated the phrase, "Biologically schizoid??"

"You know what I mean. Don't tell me you don't know what I mean."

"I *know* what you mean, Clip," Justin said with a loud whisper cloaked by the last movement of the symphony-of-the-day. "I've just never heard it exactly termed that way. And no, I don't think biologically schizoid is the deal."

"She's probably just wanting to keep your attention," Clipper said, making no sense at all, while trying to assure Justin.

Justin whispered back sarcastically, "That's a great one, Clipper."

"So, are you still on for tomorrow afternoon? If you aren't going, I can't go."

"I'm definitely on. I can't wait to get out of this town. The drive should give me time to decide what's going on with Kandi," Justin said.

The bell rang. Mr. Dumser opened his eyes and mumbled something about a discussion next class on the rise of radio. He smiled sleepily as the students exited. Justin and Clipper continued to talk as they walked into the overcrowded hallway.

"It feels weird to have all this stuff about 'See You at the Pole' floating around our school, of all places. Any more notes?"

"Nothing. You?"

"Just an E-mail. Same old stuff. It's amazing. You know I've gotten the same kind of E-mails from different addresses. Either we're being threatened by a bunch of clones, or someone's got a ton of E-mail addresses."

"What did this one say?" Clipper asked.

"No details. Just that a church was going to be destroyed. It didn't say how."

As Justin and Clipper walked down the hall negotiating their way through the turbulent stream of students, Clipper caught a glimpse of A. C. standing against the wall watching him. "Looks like I need to go see what's up with A. C."

"Where is he?" Justin searched the sea of faces.

"He's over there next to the water fountain. You don't see him?"

"Oh yeah. Want me to come with you?"

"No offense, but I don't think he'd talk to you," Clipper said. "Wow, look at that shiner."

"Looks like he's been having fun," Justin said. "Maybe you should just ignore him."

"Can't do that," Clipper said earnestly. "He might know something about these threats."

"Of course he knows something. That's what scares me," Justin replied.

Clipper smiled and shook his head. "That's what I love about you, always giving people the benefit of the doubt," Clipper said.

"See ya. Let me know what you find out about the eye," Justin said as he turned and disappeared into the throng of students.

Clipper whispered a prayer as he began making his way over to A. C., "Lord, I need some clues about these threats. Don't let me say something stupid. He'll clam up. I know he will."

"What's up?" A. C. said as Clipper walked over beside him.

"You know . . . Same stuff: term papers, athletics, pep rallies, tests, and anonymous threats that a church will be bombed. Some things never change around old Summit," Clipper said with a weak smile on his face.

"I can't believe you're laughing about it. I don't think it'll be that funny when it happens. You need to make sure all your little church friends know that this is not a joke."

"So how are you planning to do this? Do you already have the church picked out?" Clipper asked, sounding braver than he felt.

"I'm not involved, man. But you don't take this kind of stuff lightly. You should know by now that it ain't a game, Clip. Do what you have to do, but if the church goes down, you won't have anyone to blame but your own mule-headed self."

"I'm not the one in charge. If this group that you know thinks—"

"Who said I knew these folks . . . " A. C. said as he poked a finger into Clipper's chest.

"Oh give me a break! You know them," Clipper shot back.

"You never heard me say that."

"Look, Justin got a little note yesterday from this guy, van Gogh. You know that alias. We've talked about van Gogh. You've told me he was dangerous. I know he knows you, so you must know all about this," Clipper said in a tone that would have made Autumn proud.

A. C. looked away and shook his head. "I've gotta go. Just keep in mind that I'm out of the picture on this thing. I'm just trying to be a friend and tell you that you shouldn't try to make the news on this one."

As A. C. turned to leave, Clipper couldn't resist asking, "So did van Gogh give you that shiner?"

A. C. smiled, shook his head, and walked away.

Throughout the day, Autumn logically analyzed the details of the night before and concluded that she had made too much out of the whole incident. Cleary couldn't have seriously pursued her. The entire scenario made no sense. Why would a man with an incredible record, high ideals, and a bright future risk it all on a high school student? *I'm just paranoid about the situation,* she thought to herself, *especially when I already have such a high admiration for him. He's an attractive man. I need to watch my steps, and the rest will take care of itself.*

When she got home, she received a call from Melissa, a girl with whom she rarely associated. Melissa, a slightly frumpy girl, lived in one of the more well-to-do neighborhoods around Summit. She loved the telephone and took pride in knowing the private lives of her peers. Autumn had little respect for this fellow student.

"Autumn? It's Melissa. Did you see it?"

"Oh, hey, Melissa," Autumn said flatly.

"Well, did ya?" Melissa said excitedly.

"See what?"

"I hope you're not trying to be humble about the whole deal," Melissa said.

"I don't have a clue what you're talking about. What should I have seen?" Autumn said, a little frustrated.

"It's like this. I was, like, watching the soaps this morning. I've been feeling, like, totally terrible. Major headache and there was no way I was, like, going to listen to Campbell's lecture on the morality plays. I am so-o-o-o sick of the whole *everyman* deal. Like, who possibly cares about some dude looking for his purpose in life. I don't get it. You know what I mean?"

"Does this have a point?" Autumn said impatiently.

"Just hang with me for a sec," Melissa replied. "Anyway, I fell asleep in the middle of that new show, 'Lake Front Lovers.' Sherry was stranded on a cliff, but Michael was in New York having dinner with Shelly, who didn't know that Cara was really her sister's secret love. And I fell asleep because there was no way Michael could save Sherry in ten minutes. They stretch those kinds of things out for weeks. You know what I mean?"

Autumn pulled the phone away from her ear and shook her head. "So anyway, outside of the realm of the soaps, is any of this something that I'd be mildly interested in knowing?"

"Patience girl. Anyway, when I woke up, the noon report was on, and there was this politician on the news, and then they flashed your picture up on the screen and said you were, like, the youngest whatchamacallit for his thingamajig."

"On the news?" Autumn said in disbelief.

"Absolutely," Melissa said. "In front of God and everybody. I couldn't believe it. You're in the real world now. Like, go spin chick! So when did you become a . . . "

"A political whatchamacallit?"

"Yeah, that."

"I guess yesterday," Autumn said smiling. Though she had little admiration for Melissa, Autumn couldn't help being amused by her mile-a-minute mouth, her unquenchable curiosity, and her bohemian use of the English language.

"He is, like, so together. Such a major stallion! Did you just *die* when he called you? Did you just *barf* all over everything or what?"

Autumn smiled. "I don't recall barfing. No."

"I mean, when they showed footage of him, and then they showed your picture with him, I nearly fell on the floor. I just said to myself, oh my gosh! Oh my GOSH! It's, like, Autumn! I know that girl. Listen. Gotta go. Just wanted to give you the standard, 'you go, girl.' And it was great talkin' to you."

"Well, thanks," Autumn replied.

"By the way, are you, like, over what happened between us after the banquet? I was, like, a total ditz brain."

Autumn smiled and said truthfully, "Yes. I'm over it. Thanks for calling," Autumn hung up the phone and chuckled, but her mind quickly returned to the awareness that her picture appeared on the local news. She couldn't believe it. She felt a rush of adrenaline and wondered if the story would run again at six.

Her thoughts were interrupted when her father knocked on her door.

"Did you hear the news? You were on television," Rev. Sanders said with pride.

"I just heard. Did you see it?"

"I haven't seen it either. It's incredible! Fifteen people called me at the church right after the report. I knew you'd mentioned something about helping out with his campaign, but I had no idea you'd be getting exposure," Rev. Sanders said, smiling.

"Please, Dad," Autumn said seriously. "I don't like the word *exposure*. Sounds like I'm about to be on Geraldo or something."

"Speaking of Geraldo . . . Did I tell you he called?" he replied with a gleam in his eyes.

Autumn playfully batted him with her day planner.

# 10

Clipper bounced down the stairs in his house when he heard Justin's car pull into the drive, ready to head to Louisville to see Jenny.

"Hey, Justin," Clipper's dad yelled from the front door. "Clip's coming out in just a second." Clipper looked at his dad knowing that instructions would follow.

"OK. So I guess we've reached the 'threaten-the-son-within-an-inch-of-his-life' portion of the show?" Clipper said, smiling.

"How soon we grow cynical, son. I figure you've heard that speech enough, so just ponder upon the memory of that speech sometime on the road tonight. Agreed?"

"Sure," Clipper said.

"Also, just keep in mind that Jenny's vulnerable, so be careful when you talk to her."

"Don't worry, Dad. I'll be the tender man you taught me to be," Clipper said jokingly.

"OK. Just trying to keep the communication lines open. I trust you. You know that, don't you? You're a great kid. Never had any trouble with you except when you put alarm clocks in the worship center during the church business meeting."

"I've grown since then."

"Sure. Now get out of here before I change my mind," Mr. Hayes pretended to grumble. "And call us when you get to the hotel so we'll know where you're staying."

Justin and Clipper packed Justin's old Chevy Caprice and got in the car. Clipper's nervousness translated into lots of fast talk.

"Thanks for coming. I couldn't be going without you—not a chance. I'd be writing letters. And lookin' at pictures. That would be the extent of it."

"Glad to accommodate. I'm still baffled with the amount of trust your parents give me and this old boat."

"I don't get it either," Clipper admitted.

"Did they give you the third degree?"

"Not really. We're going through this trust phase. Kind of scary, really. It's kind of like I could go off the deep end and they wouldn't even know it," Clipper said.

Justin had a puzzled look on his face as he said, "And this is supposed to be a bad thing?"

"I didn't say it's bad. I just said it's scary," Clipper said as he finally buckled up.

"So what are you going to say when you get there?"

"Don't know," Clipper said as they pulled out of his driveway. "I don't know what she's going to say either. I thought she'd forgotten all about me. I mean, the relationship fizzled as far as I knew. I've been writing her all this time without any response."

"So what kind of letters did you write her? Maybe you scared her," Justin suggested.

"They weren't like that. They were just friendly, newsy letters. Not once did I say anything about love," Clipper said. "I didn't douse the envelopes in Polo. I didn't send flowers. I didn't give her cute cards with two-week-old puppies and hearts. Not romantic 'oh baby' poetry. No chocolates, no flowers, no singing telegrams. I just wrote to her about stuff. Nothing like that."

"No beanie babies?" Justin said jokingly.

"Nothing."

"How long have you been doing this?" Justin asked

"Ever since she left," Clipper replied without hesitation. "Keep in mind that my plain and simple approach took a lot of self-control. The sappy side of me was screaming to go wild with that kind of stuff, but I knew this wasn't the path that I needed to take. And I was scared out of my wits that the truth would finally come through."

"What truth?" Justin asked

"The truth that this relationship was completely over and the only thing that would happen when she returned, if she returned, is that she'd toss me an occasional smile as we passed in the halls."

"But she never called or wrote telling me to leave her alone or that she was tired of reading a narrative of my life. So I kept hoping that she still liked me. That we still had something left of the connection we had last summer. And then out of the blue, she writes me this letter as if all of a sudden our friendship has resurrected itself. More than that, she sounds like she wants more than just a surface friendship. And then I go to Mom and Dad and say, 'Hey, Mom and Dad, you remember that girl that got pregnant by some other guy while we were dating? The girl that tore my heart into little shreds? The girl that took away my desire to leave the house?' And they say, 'Why sure, son. Jenny. Right?' And I say, 'Yes. She's asked me to come over and visit her,' and they say, 'Wow, great. Go for it.'"

"I know that's not how it went," Justin said, smiling.

"Almost. I mean, here we are in a car heading for Louisville," Clipper replied.

"Pretty weird."

"Like I've said before. They really must trust us. But we've got to watch what we say. The car's probably bugged."

That afternoon, Kandi walked in her home, plopped a load of books on the kitchen table, laid down on the couch, clicked the TV on with the remote, and prepared to enter into a catatonic, post-research paper hibernation. When the phone rang, Kandi was satisfied to let the answering machine get it.

As soon as the greeting began she heard a click. The caller didn't wait to leave a message. This always unnerved Kandi, who used her machine as much to screen calls as to take messages. She turned up the TV volume. Five minutes passed. The phone rang again. The answering machine picked up, and the caller terminated the call. The next time, Kandi answered it on the first ring, her irritation apparent in her voice.

"Hey! Kandi. It's Zack."

"Zack?"

"The legendary library stalker."

"Oh," Kandi said with a light airy laugh. "I guess I do owe you an apology. So what did Mrs. Gustovson say after I left?"

"She didn't say anything. She just picked up where she left off, like nothing happened. I don't get her. She's like some kind of machine. Nothing phases her. Hey, maybe she's a scholastic terminator from the year 2130. Has anyone ever confirmed the presence of human DNA?"

"Not that I'm aware of," Kandi said. She couldn't stop smiling.

"So what's the plan?" Zack asked.

"The plan?" Kandi said, somewhat confused.

"What do you guys do in Indianapolis on the weekend?" Zack said with confidence.

"I don't understand. I mean, why are you calling me?" Kandi said.

"I just thought that maybe we could—"

"We, as in us?" Kandi said, bewildered by his straight-forward approach.

"Uh, I guess so. Unless you knew of someone else who'd want to come," Zack said.

"Like a date or something?"

"No. A date?! Ha! You thought I was calling to ask you out on a date?" Zack said, and then laughed.

"You are *really* obnoxious," Kandi said smiling. Strangely, she really enjoyed his humor and she didn't know why. If any other person had talked to her and toyed with her mind in the same way, she would have hung up the phone, but something about him made the move impossible. He had such energy and passion. He wasn't as analytical as Justin.

"I just thought it could be great to get out tonight and do some stuff."

"I don't know . . . " Kandi hesitated. Earlier in the week she had made plans to go to the movies with friends. She took a breath and expected some excuse to roll off her tongue. She had plenty to chose from, ranging from "You insolent swine. You plaster me with a balloon and then have the audacity to ask me out" to . . . "I have a boyfriend" to . . . "I'm going out with some girls to see a movie." All legitimate and true. But when she opened her mouth, what she said was, "Go out and do stuff? What kind of stuff are you talking about?"

"Just wanted to see you somewhere besides the library. No water balloons, I promise."

"I don't know."

"I promise. I'm not going to pull anything. No kissing. No holding hands. No touching. No spitting. No burping. Scout's honor. I just owe you. I really do, and my life will be totally void of meaning if I don't get the chance to make it up to you."

Autumn looked up at the clock on the wall in surprise. Had it been two hours already? Her research for Jim Cleary, though tedious, was enjoyable. She was a whiz on the Internet, and she was learning fascinating statistics about her own generation.

She had initially been hesitant when she discovered, yet again, that she and Cleary would be the only ones working late in the office. He had casually explained that he wanted the staff to have a restful weekend so they could come back Monday morning ready to hit the ground running.

Still not quite sure of the situation, Autumn had debated with herself about making up an excuse or feigning an illness so she could go back home. But she didn't want Jim to think she wasn't dependable or up for the job, so she decided to stay.

After working uninterrupted for a while, Autumn gradually dismissed her worries and immersed herself in the facts and figures in front of her.

"Need a break?" Cleary asked, stretching and rising from his desk.

"Yeah, I guess I have been pretty wrapped up in this computer," Autumn replied, straightening her back to ease the stiffness.

"Here, have a Coke. You've earned it," said Cleary as he tossed her a can from the small refrigerator near his desk. "I'm really glad you agreed to join the staff, Autumn," Cleary continued. "Without you, my platform for youth would be dead in the water."

"I guess that's a topic I'm pretty passionate about right now," Autumn said with a smile. "It seems like every time you turn on the news these days, there's been another school shooting or some kind of bomb scare. I know the answer starts at home—with the family—but if our politicians don't think it's important enough to roll up their sleeves and try to be a part of the solution, what hope is there for the future of my generation?"

Cleary looked at her and smiled. "I knew I made a good choice when I chose you to be on the staff."

Autumn tried to hide her embarrassment, but the words "when I chose you . . . " kept ringing in her head.

"And besides," Cleary added, "how many beautiful girls would give up a Friday night to sit in an office with a wannabe politician?"

Suddenly feeling very self-conscious, Autumn slowly turned to her computer screen. "I better get back to this, or I'll have to spend Saturday with you too."

"Would that be such a bad thing?" asked Cleary.

Autumn blushed in response, and gave the computer her full attention.

Later, driving home, Autumn replayed Cleary's comments in her mind. He *chose her!* And he seemed to hang on her every word when she was talking about the youth issues. Autumn was accustomed to her ideas being respected, but this was at a whole new level. Was she just being a silly teenager? She was usually able to steer clear of that sort of foolishness. A thirty-something politician flirting with her? She laughed at the absurdity of the thought.

But the way she felt when she sensed him staring at her interrupted her thoughts, as did the way he had touched her shoulder as he told her good night. She imagined what it would be like to feel that hand brush against her cheek. "Stop it! You're being ridiculous!" she said aloud, and then whispered, "Oh, Lord, please help me keep my thoughts for Jim strictly professional!"

Across town, Kandi was still in shock that she accepted Zack's invitation. She agreed to go with one simple condition—this experience would be a "nondate." Zack drove that one into the ground. "Well, for a *non*date I'm having a *non*mundane time thanks to the *non*American Chinese food with the *non*ugly, *non*boring *non*girlfriend. Let's get into the *non*Lexus and go to some undetermined *non*destination."

Kandi smiled as she got in his Jeep, "Would you please give it a rest. You've done that every time there's a lull in the conversation," she said as she buckled up and Zack started the Jeep.

"I like to refer to those lulls as *non*conversational moments," Zack replied.

"So where are we going now? It's getting kind of late. I probably need to start heading back. You know, curfew and all," Kandi said.

"No, we've got plenty of time. Gobs of time, Kandi."

"No, we really don't. I have to get home by 10:15," Kandi said.

"No, you don't," Zack said.

"Yes. I most certainly do."

"No, you don't!"

"Do!"

"In case you've forgotten, you have to be home at 11:30," Zack said. "I asked your mom."

"You asked my mom? When?"

"When you went back to your room to get your thing that you didn't have," Zack replied casually.

Kandi surrendered and looked away.

"So unless you are working as a telemarketer at home for the Chia Pet corporation, I'd say we've got plenty of time," Zack said. "I thought we were having fun."

"We were," Kandi replied. "Until I grew a conscience."

"A conscience? Whatever do you mean by that, my dear?" Zack said sarcastically.

"What I mean is—"

"What you mean is that you didn't get a signed permission slip from the guy you usually hang out with. Not that you're committed or anything. Right?"

"We're not," Kandi said with an exasperated tone. "I just think it looks bad. He's out of town and, well, it just doesn't look right."

Zack still just smiled and watched the road as he drove. Kandi stared at Zack, waiting for more. After a long pause, Zack sighed and said, "Let's get you back home. You seem to be a bit confused. And . . . "

"And what?" Kandi asked.

"And . . . I don't know. I'm not Oprah," Zack said with a smile. "I just think you are a lot of fun to be around. I wouldn't care if you were dating a gorilla. I'd still like to spend some time with you."

Kandi truly was confused. She liked Justin a lot, and yet she was also strongly attracted to Zack. He didn't have any preconceived rules or restrictions to his friendships. She didn't know anyone who lived this way. And she liked it.

In a matter of minutes they were back at Kandi's apartment complex. Kandi couldn't keep her eyes off of him. *An endangered species,* she thought to herself. *A guy who lives without an agenda.*

Early Saturday morning Clipper sat in the lobby of the Grace Home for Girls, nervously picking at a hangnail while he waited for Jenny. Justin had dropped him off a few minutes earlier with a promise to return in a couple of hours. As much as he was looking forward to his time alone with Jenny, Clipper suddenly wished for the moral support of his friend, who was headed back for the motel room. When Jenny appeared in the doorway, Clipper let out an audible gasp.

"Am I that huge?" asked Jenny, her eyes wide.

"No!" Clipper said quickly, "I'd just forgotten how beautiful you are."

Jenny's eyes dropped to look at the floor, and then turned a teary gaze back to Clipper. "I'm so glad you're here!" she said as she ran to hug him.

As he embraced her, something inside her moved. "Whoa! He just tried to belt me!" he said, jumping back.

"Well he—or *she*—is glad to see you too," Jenny laughed.

Later, as Clipper and Jenny sat on a sofa in the recreation area, Jenny broke down. "I just don't know what I'd do without you, Clipper," she sobbed. "I don't know why you're being so good to me."

Clipper was thoughtful for a moment, then spoke honestly. "Because I love you, Jenny," he finally said.

"I know you do, Clipper. That's the one thing I'm sure of right now. And that's more than I can say for anyone else," Jenny added bitterly.

"Have you heard from your parents lately?" Clipper asked, sensing the thoughts behind the dark clouds in her eyes.

"Yes, they made the obligatory weekly phone call a couple of days ago. Same old stuff. 'How are you feeling, dear?' 'Is there anything you need, dear?' 'We'll call you next week, dear.'"

Clipper tried to be encouraging, "Well, at least they call."

Jenny stood up from the couch suddenly, "Only because they feel like they have to. I know how they really feel, and I don't blame them. I've given them every reason in the world to be ashamed. Mom had to leave the room because she was sick to her stomach the night I told them. I just hope someday they can forgive me for everything." As Jenny talked, she moved over to the window.

"Forgive you? Of course they forgive you—they love you!" Clipper cried, following her to the window.

"Oh, I know they still love me in that flesh-and-blood kind of way. But I'm not sure they'll ever really feel the same about me." Jenny stared out the window at the last leaves clinging to the tree outside.

"Clipper, you're the only person I've got in my corner. And I want you to know how much that means to me. I don't know what I'd do without you."

"You don't have to worry about that Jenny. I'm with you all the way."

True to his word, Justin drove up two hours later. For Clipper, the time had gone by way too fast, but he knew he'd better get back home while he was still on his parents' good side. As Justin waited in the car, Clipper searched inside himself for the strength he needed to leave Jenny.

"I promise, I'll come up to see you again as soon as my parents will let me," Clipper said.

"We'll be here," Jenny said, patting her bulging middle.

She reached in her pocket and pulled out a white envelope with Clipper's name on it. Pressing it into his hand she pleaded, "Please don't read this until you're outside of Louisville."

"What's with the secrecy?" Clipper asked. "Are you working for the CIA now or something?"

Jenny reached out and gripped Clipper's arm with an urgency that startled him. "Clipper, I'm serious. This is important. Promise me you won't read this until you're out of town."
"OK, OK, I promise," Clipper said, not wanting to upset her.

The next thing he knew, he felt her lips brushing his, and then she turned and walked quickly down the hallway. Clipper didn't know whether to whoop with joy or cry. A honk from

Justin brought him back to reality, and he hurried out the front door with a solid resolve to come back to visit Jenny as soon as possible—if he could just convince his parents.

Two hundred miles away, A. C. stood under the dim streetlight in an old part of Indianapolis. Jazz filtered its way out of a nearby bar. He waited for the blue Camaro to appear on the corner. He shivered partly from the early fall chill and partly from the task he had decided to undertake. He wondered if he really had it in him.

After a long fifteen minutes in a subtle nighttime mist, the Camaro finally stopped in front of him.

"You comin' in?" the driver said.

A. C. felt lucky that the driver came alone.

"No, Elliot, I don't want to come in. I'd rather talk to you out here."

"It's too cold. Get in," Elliot insisted.

A. C. shook his head and said, "Not this time."

Elliot Westman turned off the ignition, perturbed by A. C.'s stubbornness. "Then spit it out. What do you want?"

"I want out of the plans," A. C. said.

"I knew we'd come to this," Elliot said. "But it's too late. We've reached the point of no return."

"I just want out. I'm not going to narc on you. Do what you want. Bomb whoever you want. I couldn't care less, but I want out of the plan," A. C. said.

Elliot lit a cigarette and shook his head. "What's your deal?"

"I'm sick to death of the game."

Elliot got out of his car and gestured for A. C. to follow him. Without a word, A. C. walked behind him. When they reached an alleyway, Elliot grabbed his arm and shoved him against the building.

"You listen to me. You want out? Fine, you're out. But no matter what happens, you keep your mouth shut. You'll be dead within twenty-four hours if you say something." Elliot pulled a small handgun out of his coat pocket and pressed it against A. C.'s neck. "You hold still. I oughta waste you right now. You are scum. I don't want you near The Association at all. You're *already* dead as far as we're concerned, and you *know* I keep my promises. We'll be watching you. If someone asks you about van Gogh, you say you never knew him. Right?"

A. C. numbly nodded his head, trying to swallow the knot of fear in his throat.

Kandi stared at the TV, but her mind definitely wasn't on the Saturday morning cartoons that scampered around on the screen. Instead, her thoughts kept going back to the night before with Zack. It had been harmless enough—and much to her surprise, she had really enjoyed herself.

*Then why do I feel so guilty?* Kandi wondered. *Because you're supposed to be dating Justin, stupid!* she answered herself.

There had been a message on the answering machine from Justin when she had arrived home the night before. He sounded pretty lonely calling from their hotel room, even though she could hear Clipper sending her greetings in the background. Her heart sunk as she listened to the message. How would she explain to Justin where she had been on a Friday night or who she had been with?

Just then the shrill sound of the doorbell interrupted her thoughts. *Great!* she thought. *No makeup and I'm still in my pajamas.*

When she got to the door, a huge bouquet of flowers greeted her—with a deliveryman peering around them. Kandi did a quick mental check to think of who might be sending flowers to her mother. Her father, recovering from a near-fatal car wreck, came to mind. *No, he's changed, but not enough to send flowers to his ex-wife.*

After signing for them and thanking the deliveryman, Kandi carried them into the kitchen. A small, pink envelope was tucked in between some baby's breath and daisies. It had Kandi's name on it.

*For me?! Maybe they are from Daddy,* thought Kandi as she tore open the envelope.

> *Kandi,*
> *Thank you for being willing to be seen with me in public last night.*
> *Zack*

Kandi re-read the note to make sure she wasn't dreaming. *Flowers? He sent me flowers?* she thought, a slow warmth spreading over her.

The phone ringing brought her back to reality. *Omigosh! Justin!* she panicked, feeling the guilt surge back in.

"Hello?"

"So did you like the flowers?" a cocky voice on the other end asked.

"Zack!"

"The one and only."

"Why did you . . . I mean, why would you . . . I . . . um, yes. Yes, I love the flowers. They're beautiful. But . . . why?"

"I don't know. I just got up this morning and thought 'Hey, why not boost the floral economy?' You were the only person whose address I knew."

"Zack . . . " the frustration in her voice was evident through the phone line.

"I'm just kidding! I just wanted to send you flowers. Is that a crime?"

"No . . . I'm sorry. They really are beautiful."

"Good. Well, gotta run. 'Scooby Doo' is on!"

Click. He was gone. Kandi stood, still holding the receiver in one hand, stunned by the morning's events. *What nerve!* she thought. *He definitely has a super-size ego!* But then she got another glimpse of the flowers, sitting on the kitchen table, and suddenly she started to laugh. "I've got to hand it to him," she said to the empty house, "he definitely knows how to leave an impression!"

Clipper and Justin had ridden in silence for many miles. Justin knew his friend well enough to leave him to his thoughts. He could tell from the look on Clipper's face that the conversation with Jenny must have been pretty intense. He wanted to ask a hundred questions, but he knew that would come later.

As he left Clipper to sort through the morning's events from the passenger seat, Justin's thoughts turned to Kandi. *Why did all their conversations end in petty arguments lately?* It had gotten to the point where he sometimes dreaded calling her. Of course, last night he had tried to call her, only to find her not home. *Where was she on a Friday night?* Justin wondered. He knew Autumn was spending all her spare time over at that Cleary guy's office, so Kandi couldn't have been with her. He normally wasn't the jealous type, but there had been so much tension lately, it made him nervous to consider Kandi's Friday night options.

Kandi had been dealing with so much lately—moving to a new town, trying to make new friends, and then an alcoholic father on top of all that. *Maybe I should cut her some slack,* Justin thought.

As Justin contemplated how to repair his relationship with Kandi, Clipper was trying to decide how to convince his parents to let him come back to see Jenny the next weekend. *Surely they'll let me come back when I tell them how lonely she is,* he thought. Jenny's tear-filled eyes flashed before him again, and Clipper had to stare intently out the window to keep his own eyes from misting.

The moment he was certain they were outside Louisville, Clipper took the letter from his pocket. He had checked it every minute or so to be certain he had not lost it going from the building to the car. As Clipper opened the letter, Justin shot him a curious look, which Clipper ignored. He caught a whiff of Jenny's scent as he unfolded the paper, and he had to blink a few times to be able to focus on what she'd written.

*Dear Clipper,*

*If you're reading this, then that means you've just visited me. Let me say again how much that means to me. I get so lonely here sometimes, I think I'll go crazy. I know I got myself into this mess, so I guess I shouldn't complain. I just miss seeing you.*

*You are the most insane, wonderful thing that has ever happened to me. For the first time, I know what real love feels like. And I want you to know that I love you too, Clipper.*

*I know this is going to sound crazy, but I've been thinking about keeping my baby. Now don't freak, but I've also been*

*thinking about what a great father you'd make. I know we're*
*young, but I think we could make it work. That is, if you'd con-*
*sider marrying me. I can't believe I'm even writing you this! I*
*just think we could really make a great family.*

    *Look, if I don't hear back from you, I'll totally understand.*
*I hope, though, that you'll still be my friend. If you don't think*
*I've completely lost it, then I hope I'll hear from you soon.*

    *Love,*
    *Jenny*

    "Whoa!" Clipper couldn't help letting out an audible sigh.

    "What's up?" Justin asked, unable to suppress his questions
any longer.

    "Um . . . just a letter from Jenny."

    "Gee, didn't you guys just see each other?"

    "Yeah, but you know how girls are," Clipper said, reaching
over and turning the radio up.

    Justin could tell that the conversation had just been halted,
so he turned his thoughts back to the road ahead, figuring
Clipper would eventually tell him what was going on.

# 15

When Kandi's doorbell rang late that afternoon, she seriously considered sneaking out the rear window of the apartment. She wanted time alone, not another interpersonal chess match. Kandi plastered on a tight smile when she saw Justin.

"Well, can I come in, or do I need a written invitation?" Justin asked, trying a half-hearted joke.

"Oh! I'm sorry, come on in." Slightly flustered, Kandi led him inside and motioned for him to sit on the couch. Kandi sat in the recliner across the room.

"Hello, Justin," Kandi's mother stuck her head out of her bedroom. "I was beginning to wonder why I hadn't seen you this weekend."

"I went to Louisville overnight with Clipper so he could visit Jenny."

"How is she? I ran into her mother the other day, but she didn't bring the subject up. I figured I better not either."

"I'm not sure how she is. Clipper didn't seem to want to talk about it in the car on the way back. I think he was pretty bummed about having to leave her behind," Justin replied.

Kandi hoped her mother would join them in the den so she wouldn't have to be alone with Justin, but just as quickly as she had stuck her head in, her mother excused herself and disappeared back into the bedroom.

Not quite knowing what to say, Kandi asked, "So you had a good trip then?"

"I guess. Basically we just drove there, spent the night, and then drove back. I tried to call you last night from the hotel, but you weren't home."

Kandi wanted to kick herself for leading Justin down that path of conversation. "Oh, yeah. I'm sorry I missed your call. I went out for a little while." *Please drop it, Justin!* Kandi willed him from her side of the den.

They made small talk for a while, then finally settled back into being comfortable with each other. They discussed the mysterious letter Clipper got from Jenny and theorized what might be in it. They talked about school and the latest "See You at the Pole" threat.

After they talked awhile, Justin asked if he could have a Coke. Despite Kandi's protests that she didn't need his help, Justin followed her into the kitchen. While she fixed both of them glasses of Coke, Justin noticed the flowers on the table. "Nice," he offered nonchalantly.

"They are pretty, aren't they?" Kandi replied, nearly spilling her Coke on the floor.

"Boy, somebody must have some money to burn," said Justin.

Kandi spun around to face him. "Maybe *some* people *like* to spend money on others," she replied hotly.

"OK, Kandi, what's going on?" he demanded.

"What are you talking about?" she stalled.

"You're acting so distant. And incredibly defensive about the flowers. Where did they come from?" Justin asked.

"Just some guy I know. He's just a friend," Kandi answered.

"Friends don't buy friends flowers. Who *is* he?" Justin asked again, assertively.

"His name is Zack."

"Zack? Zack Galloway?"

"Yes. But we are friends. Which is something you're having trouble being . . ." Kandi responded, still angry. "Maybe this isn't a good time for us to visit."

"Where were you last night?"

"Who are you? My personal interrogator?" Kandi knew she was caught. She didn't want to lie to Justin, but she resented his sudden possessiveness. "Look, I went out last night—just as friends—with Zack from school. He just sent the flowers this morning as kind of a . . . thank you."

"You went out with another guy last night?!" Justin exclaimed.

"Well, you were out of town, and I really wanted to go do something. Is that so wrong for a teenage girl to want to go out on a Friday night?"

"Please, Kandi! I was doing Clipper a favor! Are you going to penalize me for helping a friend?"

Kandi stared at the floor. She knew there was no way she could justify going out with Zack. "I'm sorry Justin. He was just so persistent . . . and I didn't think it would hurt just to go do something with him. The flowers were a total shock. I had no idea he'd do something like that."

Justin swallowed hard. "What's going on with us?" he asked. "Lately all we seem to do is argue . . . and now this. Have I done something? Do you like this Zack guy?"

"No, no," Kandi fought back tears. "It's my fault. I don't know what's the matter with me." The tears were falling unhindered now. "I just feel like I don't know what I want right now."

Justin stood watching her, then he quietly asked, "So what does that mean for us exactly?"

"I don't know. I just feel like maybe it would be better if we were just friends for right now, until I can sort things out."

"If that's the way you feel, I guess there's not a whole lot I can say." He touched her arm for a second. "But I'm still here for you if you need me."

"I know you are."

After Justin left, Kandi sat at the kitchen table, staring at the flowers in front of her. She jumped when a load of laundry suddenly landed on the floor beside her.

"Sorry, didn't mean to startle you," her mom apologized. "You sure were deep in thought. Did something happen with Justin?"

"I'm not sure, but I think it's over."

"Do you want to talk about it?"

"Thanks, Mom, maybe tomorrow. I don't think I'm up to it tonight."

"OK, but if you change your mind, I'm here."

"I love you, Mom."

"I love you too, sweetie."

While her mom finished sorting the laundry, Kandi went back over her conversation with Justin. She had been quick to deny any interest in Zack, but his face kept popping into her head. *Do I have feelings for Zack?*

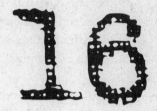

Autumn usually loved to hear her father preach, but this Sunday morning she was having a tough time keeping her mind on the sermon outline. She couldn't even keep her mind on the conversation she'd had with Eli before church. Instead, she kept thinking about Jim Cleary.

Autumn was already planning her schedule for the next week and calculating how much time she could devote to the campaign. While she made certain that she kept up with her studies, more often she found herself rushing through an assignment so she could head over to the campaign headquarters. *I'm turning into a real mouse potato,* Autumn thought to herself. But she reasoned that this campaign could do more to boost her future than any calculus assignment could.

Later, Autumn helped her mom and dad clear away the dishes. Her mother, though a busy woman, always made a point to serve a big meal on Sundays after church.

As the last dish was going into the dishwasher, Autumn's mother broached the subject that had been bothering her earlier.

"Is everything going well at school?" she asked.

"Sure. I'm expecting A's in all my classes this report period. Why?"

"You just seem like you've got a lot on your mind lately. You don't think working on Mr. Cleary's campaign is stretching you too thin, do you?"

"No!" Autumn was quick to answer, "I mean . . . I've been a lot busier since I started working with Jim, but . . . "

"Jim?"

"I mean . . . Mr. Cleary. But I don't think it's any more than I can handle."

Autumn hoped her confidence had been convincing. She knew what her mother was getting at, but she didn't know how to explain to her the confusing feelings she'd been having. Her mother would probably think she had a crush on Cleary and make her quit working on the campaign.

Autumn didn't like keeping things from her parents. But even worse to her was the humiliating thought of having to tell Jim Cleary that her parents didn't want her to work on the campaign any further. This scenario convinced her to keep quiet for now. *Besides, there's really nothing to tell anyway,* Autumn thought to herself.

"I hate Mondays," Clipper announced as he banged his locker door shut.

"What?" Justin replied, "Mr. Glass-is-always-half-full suddenly hates Mondays? What's with you?"

"It's just the same old boring routine, week after week, year after year. Aren't you ready to get on with your life?"

"What are you talking about? College? We'll be there soon enough."

"No, no. That's not what I mean. I'm talking about doing something worthwhile . . . getting married and having a family."

"Whoa! Where'd that come from?" Justin asked, shock registering on his face.

"I don't know," Clipper said, suddenly wishing he'd kept his mouth shut.

"Well, after this weekend, marriage is a four-letter word in my dictionary," said Justin.

"Why? What happened?" asked Clipper, grateful for the shift in conversation.

"Basically, Kandi and I have decided to just 'be friends.'"

"Oooooh! Talk about your old relationship kiss of death!"

"No way! I don't know what's going on with her right now, but I meant it when I told her I'd still be here for her. Whether we're dating or not, I really care about her," Justin added defensively.

Clipper threw up his hands in mock surrender. "Hey! I'm not the enemy, remember?" After a moment, he added, "I know what you mean about being there for her. I feel the same way about Jenny. Even though we're not dating, I'd still do anything for her." *But would I marry her?* Clipper thought to himself.

"Well, if it isn't the gruesome twosome!" Autumn laughed as she walked up to their lockers.

"And if it isn't Summit High's own personal lobbyist!" retorted Justin. "Long time no see!"

"Yeah, I know. This campaign is keeping me pretty busy. I heard you guys went to see Jenny this weekend. How's she holding up?"

"She's pretty lonely. I'm planning to go back and see her as soon as possible—one way or another," replied Clipper.

Autumn and Justin exchanged concerned glances.

"And how's Kandi?" Autumn said to Justin. "I didn't talk to her this weekend."

"Long story," Justin replied distantly.

"I ran into Eli this morning, and he told me that some guy named Zack told him—"

"Zack?!" Justin interrupted, nearly shouting.

Autumn immediately knew that she'd said the wrong thing. "Who's Zack?"

"Nobody. Never mind," and Justin turned on his heel and headed for class.

"What's going on?" Autumn asked Clipper. "I get the distinct impression that Justin doesn't care for Zack too much."

"I'm not sure. Justin's closed off to everybody lately. I try to talk to him about Kandi, and he's like the smoking man from the *X Files*. No facts—just lots of strange implications. The truth *is* out there."

"You're strange."

"Thanks, Autumn," Clipper said proudly. "So how is that going, working with a bunch of liars and crooks?"

"Clip! Get out!" Autumn gave him an angry wallop.

"Sorry! Geesh, I was just joking! Calm down!"

Autumn was surprised at how vehemently she had just defended this man whom she hardly knew. "I'm sorry, I . . . I just really believe in Jim and the things he stands for. Oh, I almost forgot! Watch the news tonight, and you may catch a glimpse of us. We're having a press conference this afternoon at the campaign headquarters."

"Hey, I dare you to make rabbit ears behind Cleary while he's talking! 'TV Bloopers and Practical Jokes' will be waiting."

"Clipper, you're hopeless."

Autumn got an excuse from her parents to leave school early to attend the press conference. As she pulled into the parking lot of the campaign headquarters, she saw several news crews setting up their equipment.

Autumn felt a rush of adrenaline as she parked her car and started walking toward the office. Several reporters glanced in her direction, then went back to their preparations for the conference.

In the office, there was a flurry of activity. Not quite knowing what to do, Autumn stood in the doorway for a moment.

Cleary looked up from the notes he was taking and gave her a broad grin. "Autumn! Great! Now the gang's all here. Let me go over these notes one more time, and then let's get this show on the road."

Fifteen minutes later they all assembled outside the headquarters. Autumn tried to make herself as inconspicuous as possible by blending in with the other staffers.

When Cleary began his remarks, Autumn glowed with pride. He really is a great orator, she thought, admiringly. Suddenly her thoughts were interrupted as she heard her name.

" . . . whom I'd like to introduce as the first fully active campaign staff member who is still in high school. It was Autumn's passion for education reform and teen issues that has helped shaped my campaign. She has proven to be a valuable member of our team. Autumn, step up here and wave to the crowd," Cleary beckoned.

Autumn had been in front of crowds before, but this time she almost felt sick. With as much poise as she could muster, she stepped forward, smiled, and waved to the reporters. Several shouted out questions related to teen violence statistics. Cleary motioned for her to take the mike, which she did only after forcing her stomach out of her throat. Autumn managed to field every question with a maturity and assurance belying her age.

The reporters were obviously smitten with the teenager. One shouted to Cleary, "So how does it feel to have a political prodigy on your staff?"

"Better my staff than Lindsay's!" Cleary laughed. "But in all seriousness, having Autumn on my staff helps me keep it real. I mean, truly, the answer to teen violence starts at home—with the family—but if we as politicians don't think it's important enough to roll up our sleeves and try to be a part of the solution, what hope is there for the future of Autumn's generation?"

The crowd burst into spontaneous applause. *That's what I said to him the other night!* Autumn thought to herself. She could barely contain her growing excitement that Cleary had quoted *her* in his remarks—and had gotten applause too!

18

After all the reporters had left, Cleary and his staff celebrated inside the campaign headquarters. The atmosphere was charged with excitement as staffers gave each other congratulatory high-fives at the success of the press conference.

Everyone gathered around the television when the newscast began. A holdup at a local convenience store. A drive-by shooting had left one person seriously injured. "And in other news today, senatorial candidate Jim Cleary held a press conference this afternoon to discuss the need for government to get more involved in the teen violence issue . . ." The staff cheered as they watched.

And then there he was, looking every bit as handsome on television as he did in real life, Autumn noticed. And they were showing him making the comments where he was quoting her! *This day just can't get any better!* Autumn thought. *I hope my parents are watching.* Autumn looked up and caught Jim looking at her. He mouthed the words "thank you" to her. She smiled and nodded, then went back to watching the rest of the newscast.

After the news ended, the staff sat around for a while and made lofty predictions of how badly Cleary would defeat Senator Lindsay. Cleary made sure to steer clear of making any such suggestions, but he obviously enjoyed the conversation.

Autumn got her things together, explaining with some embarrassment that it was a school night. They gave her some good-natured ribbing and bid her good night.

"I'll walk you to your car since it's dark out," Cleary offered.

Although Autumn didn't really see the need for an escort, she didn't refuse his company walking out to the parking lot.

"You know," Cleary said, "I meant every word of what I said today. You are a very valuable member of this campaign."

Autumn felt herself blush. "Thanks, Jim. I'm really enjoying working with you—and the staff," Autumn added quickly.

Before she knew what was happening, Jim had taken her in his arms and was kissing her. At first, Autumn melted into the moment, finally realizing those things that she had only imagined before.

But something inside her screamed, *This is wrong!* Like she had an electrical current running through her, Autumn jumped back. Cleary gave her a surprised look.

"It's OK, Autumn. No one can see us out here." He reached to embrace her again.

Autumn took a step back and sat down in the driver's seat of her car. "I'm sorry, Jim, but it's not OK." She shut the door with as much grace as she could and quickly started the car and drove off.

*Lord, what did I do to bring that on?* she cried.

Autumn's mother found her sitting outside on the porch swing. "What's the matter?" she asked when she noticed Autumn's tears.

As much as she wanted to, Autumn could not tell her mother what had happened, not yet anyway. She had to sort through how, and why, all this had happened. "I don't know, Mom. It's just that nothing seems to be going like I thought it would."

Autumn's mother smiled. "That's a common problem with life, honey."

"I know. But things were going so well working on Jim's campaign—he even quoted something I'd said to him on the evening news tonight!"

"I thought those words sounded like something you'd come up with. Why didn't he give you credit?"

"I don't know. And that's not what's important. What's important is that he thought I, Autumn Sanders, was worth quoting."

"Well, then, what's the problem?" Mrs. Sanders continued to press.

"It's just . . . it's just more complicated than I thought it was going to be," Autumn hedged once again.

"You know, a lot of times, success seems so easy or so important. Yet, once you achieve it, you're left with a mysterious hollowness. Just remember that there's only One who can calm the chaos and fill that emptiness you're feeling."

"I know, Mom, I know."

Mother and daughter sat there, just being silent together, each wondering what she could do to calm the other's worries.

Monday afternoon, Kandi's biggest concern was an English assignment due by the end of the week. Books lay open in front of her, but creativity just waved from a distance.

When the doorbell rang, she almost jumped out of her skin. Not knowing what to say if Justin were standing there, Kandi approached the door with a small amount of dread. Instead, it was Zack, with the usual smirk on his face.

With a mixture of annoyance and relief, Kandi opened the door to greet him. "Zack! What are you doing here?"

"I came to see if you could come out and play," Zack replied nonchalantly.

Kandi had to laugh at his boldness, but she didn't buy into the act. "I've told you, I can't go out on a date with you."

"Well, Miss High and Mighty, who said anything about a date? I want to take you on a history lesson."

Feeling a little sheepish at her assumption, she questioned

him further. "What are you talking about, a history lesson?"

"Crown Hill Cemetery."

Zack had successfully intrigued her. Kandi sat quietly as they drove to the cemetery and made their way to the entrance.

As they approached the massive iron gates of Crown Hill Cemetery, Zack stepped to one side and took on the role of tour guide.

"And here, ladies and gentleman, is the third largest cemetery in the country." With a grand flourish of his arms, he waved Kandi through the entrance.

"How did you know that? About it being the third largest in the country?" she asked.

"Oh, I dunno. You might say cemeteries are my hobby."

"Gee, do you think you could pick something a little less morbid?"

"Morbid? There're some fascinating people six feet under. Look over here, for instance. Here lies that famous criminal John Dillinger. You've read all about his exploits, but here you get to see him in person—so to speak," Zack added with a wink.

Kandi was amazed. Sure enough, there on the tombstone read "John Dillinger."

"So, you got any other friends up here you'd like me to meet?" she asked with a playful grin.

In spite of herself, Kandi found she was having fun. They spent the afternoon going from grave to grave looking at names and dates. She couldn't believe how old some of the markers were. It struck her as odd that someone like Zack, so full of life, could be so fascinated by death.

"So how did you come upon this, um, hobby?" she asked.

"Well, I guess I was just curious about what happens to us after we die. This seemed the natural place to come."

Something besides the autumn wind in the cemetery made Kandi shiver. "Well, I don't know about you, but I intend to wind up in heaven." She knew Shawn, her youth pastor, would laugh at her lame attempt to work in the gospel.

"Heaven Shmeven. You really believe in that stuff, huh?" Zack said.

"Yeah, I do. I take it that you don't?" Kandi said inquisitively.

"I don't know. I hope there's a heaven, but I never have been very much on conventional theology. I'm more of a Dylan Thomas guy myself. Great dead poet. One of the best." Suddenly he jumped on top of one of the broad granite memorial stones and began to recite the words of Thomas, "'Do not go gently into that good night. Old age may burn a rage at close of day. Rage! Rage against the dying of the light.'" Zack said.

Kandi laughed in disbelief. "Get down before we get arrested!"

Zack hopped down and continued. "But you. Now you are a toughie. You are too cautious. You think too much. Don't get me wrong. I re-e-e-e-eally like you, but, shweetheart, sometimes you jusht have to enjoy the moment and forget about what other people think. 'Hold onto sixteen as long as you can.' That's Mellencamp, by the way. You've chosen the straight and narrow, though. I can see you now—Saint Kandi—floating around the clouds playing your harp!" He threw some leaves at her, and then ran off to another section of the cemetery.

Kandi didn't know what to make of his irreverence, but his honesty and no-holds-barred way of looking at things energized her. She found herself laughing as she ran after him with a huge armful of leaves for retaliation.

# 20

By Tuesday evening, Clipper had thought about Jenny until he was nearly delirious. He couldn't get her letter out of his mind. How could he? This wasn't your average teenage "if you like me, check yes" note she'd written. This was probably the biggest thing he had ever faced.

His parents noticed his distraction the moment he returned from Louisville, but they had attributed it to his angst at leaving Jenny behind. Clipper knew his parents would go ballistic if they even suspected what he was contemplating.

He picked up the phone dozens of times to call Jenny, but he had hung up every time. *What can I say to her?* he wondered. *I'm only a teenager. But how can I tell Jenny no?*

He went outside and tried to shoot hoops. He found himself thinking how great it would be if Jenny had a boy, and he could teach him to play basketball. *Are you crazy?* he asked himself. *She hasn't even had the baby yet, and you're already preparing the kid for the NBA.*

Clipper went back inside and tried to watch television. Still, not even reruns of *Saved by the Bell* could keep his mind off his dilemma. *This is ridiculous,* Clipper thought to himself. *No sense putting this off any longer.* He reached for the phone and dialed the number in Kentucky.

The phone rang and rang. Clipper was just about to chicken out and hang up when someone answered. He asked to speak to Jenny, and then held his breath while he waited for her to come to the phone. He didn't have to wait long.

"Hello?" Jenny said.

"Hello, beautiful," Clipper answered, nearly choking with emotion at hearing her voice.

"Clipper?!" Jenny exclaimed with obvious apprehension.

"Look, I know we've both been thinking about this since I left you Saturday, so let me get to the point."

He could hear Jenny catch her breath. "It's OK. Don't worry about it."

"Jenny, will you marry me?"

Jenny sat silent for a moment on the other end. "Did you just say what I think you just said?" she asked finally.

"If you still want me, that is," said Clipper.

"Oh, Clipper! Of course I still want to marry you! I can't believe this!" She began to cry.

"It's all I've thought about, Jenny. Listen, what if we wait until a couple of months after the baby is born and then get married?"

"That's perfect! That will give me a chance to shed a few pounds of 'baby fat' before the wedding. Oh, Clipper, I knew you'd come through for me!"

"Jenny, one thing. I've got to know that you're in this for the long haul—not just so you can keep the baby. I've always said that when I get married, it's going to be for life."

Jenny tried hard not to sound hurt by his words. "Clipper, of course I'm in it forever. You know I love you."

Clipper immediately felt bad for doubting her, "I'm sorry, I just had to make sure."

"When do you think we should tell our parents?" asked Jenny.

"Probably not until the baby gets here; otherwise, we'll just have to put up with more grief. I'm sure once they see the baby, they'll just be a puddle of grandparenting." Clipper laughed at the thought, *My mom, a grandma!*

Autumn dove into her homework that night. She had spent so much time on Cleary's campaign that she was now juggling several school projects. She didn't mind though. It gave her the perfect out to honestly ask for time away from the campaign. As soon as the phone beside her computer rang, she answered it, without even thinking that it might be Cleary.

"Hello?"

"Autumn, Jim Cleary here."

"Hello, Jim," Autumn replied nervously.

"Look, I missed seeing you at the office this afternoon. You aren't sick, are you?"

"No, I just had a lot of school stuff I had to do. I'm sorry if it caused any problems."

"No, no problem, I was just worried about you." Cleary coughed and then continued, "Look, I want to apologize for what happened last night. I shouldn't have surprised you like that."

Autumn struggled for something to say. She hadn't expected him to be so up front about the whole situation, but at least he was apologizing. "I accept your apology. I'm sorry I ran off the way I did. You just . . . caught me off guard."

"I was puzzled that you took off like that. I know I'm no DiCaprio, but I didn't expect you to bolt," he laughed.

Autumn wondered what he had expected her response to be, but she kept her question to herself.

"Autumn, I promise not to surprise you any more if you'll continue to work with me on the campaign."

"This isn't one of those campaign promises, is it?" Autumn asked, still not sure of the situation.

"No, I mean it. No more surprises. Just please come back to work."

Later that evening, Autumn sat wondering if she'd done the right thing. She told Cleary that she'd be at the campaign head-quarters tomorrow after school. He had assured her that there would be several other staff members there, which had put her mind somewhat at ease.

"Phone for you," her mother called from the next room.

*Oh no,* Autumn thought. *What does he want now?*

To her surprise, she heard Eli on the other end of the line.

"Hey! I can't believe I actually caught you at home," he began. "I called to see if you wanted to ride to youth group with me tomorrow night."

"Um . . . I'm not sure. I mean, I'd love to, but I'm supposed to go work over at Cleary's office tomorrow after school. I'm not sure I'll be done in time to get to church."

Eli was unable to hide the irritation in his voice. "Well, I wouldn't want to do anything to stop the great political machine!"

"What's that supposed to mean?"

"It means that you're still in high school, remember? You're entitled to have some fun. Lately all you do is sit around playing politics with that Cleary guy."

Autumn could feel her blood beginning to boil. "That 'Cleary guy' is going to be your next senator if I have anything to do with it! And excuse me if I have more important things to do with my time than to sit around and wait for you to call!" She slammed down the phone.

"Everything OK?" her mother asked cautiously, peeking around her door.

"Yes," Autumn answered, still angry over Eli's comments. "Just confirmation of what I've always said—relationships are not my thing!"

When Clipper walked in the door from school the next day, he found a note for him attached to the refrigerator: "Call Jenny. Urgent." Clipper nearly tripped over his own feet trying to hurry to the phone. A million thoughts raced through his head as he waited for someone to answer. Maybe she's had a change of heart about marrying me. *Maybe her parents have found out our plan and are coming to kill me . . .*

"Hello," a female voice answered.

"Yes, I'm calling for Jenny Elton, please."

"Just a moment."

The woman put him on hold. While he waited for Jenny to answer, Clipper continued to panic over why she would call him like that. *She knew I'd be in school, so why would she call during the day like that?* He also began to concoct a scheme to elope if, indeed, Jenny's parents had found out and were against their marrying.

"Hello, Clipper?" Jenny sounded very tired and weak. Clipper's heart raced even faster.

"What's the matter Jenny? The message my mom left said it was urgent."

He could hear Jenny softly crying over the phone. "The doctor says my blood pressure is really high. My legs and ankles are starting to swell. He's making me stay in bed for the rest of the week. He says if things don't change, he's going to have to put me in the hospital, and maybe to bed for the rest of my pregnancy. I'm so scared!"

While worried about Jenny and the baby, Clipper was relieved that he wasn't going to have to dodge bullets from Jenny's father—yet. "Gee, I wish somebody would tell me to stay in bed all the time. That's the one thing I'm pretty good at!" Clipper tried to joke. When he noticed that his attempt at humor wasn't working, he turned more serious, "Hey, I'm sorry Jenny. I was just kidding. What do your parents have to say?"

"They told me they were sorry and just to do what the doctor told me."

"Well, aren't they going to come see you? Check on you?"

"If they are, they didn't tell me," Jenny replied bitterly. She started to cry even harder. "I'm sure they think this is just one more thing I've gotten myself in to. I'm so scared, Clipper . . . " her sobs kept her from continuing.

"Jenny, I'm going to come see you this weekend, OK? Do you think you can hang in there until then?"

Jenny calmed down some at the idea of Clipper visiting again. They talked a few minutes more, then hung up, both of them thinking about seeing each other again.

*I don't know how I'm going to talk my parents into this one, Lord. But I've just got to see Jenny.*

That same evening Autumn sat in front of her laptop attempting to block out the events of the past twenty-four hours. But as she often did, she found herself journaling the events, hoping that if she could spill her emotions on the keyboard they wouldn't invade her dreams that night. She flinched at the sound of the telephone and prayed the call wasn't for her. She just wanted to retreat from human contact for a while. A few moments later her father knocked on the door.

"Autumn? You in there? It's the *Post* wanting a little information about your relationship with that politician," Rev. Sanders said.

Her heart hit the floor until he started to chuckle. "Funny, Dad." She imagined what he'd think if he only knew.

"Seriously, it's Kandi," he said.

Autumn picked up the phone and waited for her dad to hang up. She greeted Kandi with a simple, "Hey," still waiting for the click. She cupped the mouthpiece and then called to her dad, "Got it, Dad. You can hang up."

"Sounding a little paranoid, Autumn," Kandi said.

"It's becoming a way of life," Autumn said.

"What?" Kandi asked.

"Oh, nothing. Forget I said that. Just a tad stressed out."

Kandi sighed and began a frequent lecture, "You know high ambitions and no leisure will do that to you."

"So what's going on?"

"Just a lot of junk. I seem to attract it these days," Kandi said in a downcast voice.

"Join the club."

"Really?" Kandi asked. "Like what?"

"You first."

"Justin and I flamed out," Kandi said. "You know how I told you the other day that things had gotten stale between us. I think I can now say that they've gone from stale to rotten."

Autumn was stunned. "What happened?"

"It's over," Kandi said dryly. "And the worst thing about it is that I'm totally numb."

"Oh, Kandi. I'm so sorry," Autumn said.

"I guess I must have wanted it to be over because I didn't exactly throw a fit about it all. One minute we were feeling awkward and the next minute he turned suspicious, and that's when I got mad. He saw some flowers that Zack—"

Autumn flipped. "Zack! Zack gave you flowers!"

"Yes. But it wasn't like I did anything to provoke them. Justin came over and he became very nosey and defensive, just a few of my least favorite qualities in a guy, and the next thing

I know we're in a debate with my mom probably hearing every word from the next room. It was really embarrassing.

"So now we're doing the friends deal, and you know what that means. We'll see each other and frown a lot and before we know it, we'll be avoiding each other, developing cute little nicknames for each other like creep, dirt bag, and high and mighty," Kandi sighed. "So that's my story. What's yours?"

"That's, uh, quite a little summation there, girl. In less than five hundred words. So tell me about Zack," Autumn asked curiously.

"Long, complex story. I want to hear about you, though," Kandi said.

Autumn paused, fighting the urge to lie about the cause of her strange disposition. *I really need to talk to someone about all this,* she thought to herself. "Please, Kandi. I guess I should let you in on this."

"Uh-oh. You're serious. What is it?"

"It's about Cleary," Autumn said, then paused.

"OK," Kandi said, a leading lilt in her voice.

"The whole thing is getting weird," Autumn said, and then was quiet again.

"Autumn! Spit it out. We've got school in a few hours," Kandi said impatiently.

"The facts don't make the whole story. That's why this is so hard to explain. I've had this feeling for the past week that Cleary looks at me differently than he does the others. He'd asked me to come work with the team. I get there and guess what? No team. It's just me and Cleary. I'll catch him watching me. Maybe it's normal. You've had lots more experience handling these situations than I have, but to me it seemed more than just an innocent stare. I mean, I love the man. Wait. I take that back. I love working for the man."

"You think he's coming on to you?" Kandi probed.

"He'd make flattering comments about me, my hair, how much he enjoyed being around me."

"He's a politician, Autumn. That's kind of his forte," Kandi said jokingly,

"That's not all. A couple of days ago I was working in his office. He comes up from behind me and starts to rub my shoulders. All very innocent sounding. You know. Saying how tense I was and how he appreciated my overtime. It's not like sexual harassment because, to tell you the truth, I've been, well, attracted to him. Not seriously but I think—"

"That he's a very powerful, handsome guy and that it's safe to have those kinds of feelings because you're just a high school student and what's even more implausible is that you think it's more than the age factor. There's the race factor," Kandi said.

"Absolutely. How far fetched would that be for a public figure? There's no way, I thought. I mean, we're in the new millennium but racists vote too, so why would the urge even manifest itself in Cleary?"

"OK. So far we have a politician and an aspiring masseuse," Kandi said.

"You really are getting good at these summaries," Autumn said. She could feel her heart accelerate as she anguished about whether to continue the truth telling. "Then there was the kiss."

"THE KISS?"

"Please, Kandi. You can't tell anyone."

"I was only planning to tell Melissa," Kandi said.

"Funny. That's really funny, Kandi," Autumn hissed.

"I'm sorry. It's just my way of dealing with total shock. You mean a *kiss* kiss. On the mouth? When?"

"Suffice it to say that he kissed me, and I kissed back for a moment until reality set in, and I bolted out of there."

"You kissed back, huh?" Kandi said with a mixture of giddiness and perplexity.

"You can't, cannot, absolutely can't, tell anyone. Not your mom, not Justin . . . "

"Autumn, we went through this. It'll go to the grave with me."

"You aren't planning to come back from the dead, are you?" Kandi laughed.

"What do I do? He apologized and said he was in the wrong and that he wanted me to stay on board. I don't know. This assignment has been like a dream and now—"

Kandi interrupted. "Autumn, he's a big boy. I'd give him a break. You are always denying that you have a certain attraction to guys. I think this just proves what I've been telling you—you are a babe."

"GET OUT!" Autumn said loudly.

"I'm sorry. I couldn't resist."

# 25

At school the next day, Autumn's preoccupation with the campaign job escalated. She changed her mind a dozen times about whether she should go to the campaign office that afternoon. By the time the final bell sounded, the only thing Autumn knew for certain was that she needed to talk to someone.

Mrs. Moore smiled broadly as her favorite debate student walked into the classroom, but her smile quickly faded when she saw the look on Autumn's face.

"What's wrong?" she asked as she stood up from her desk.

"I'm not sure," Autumn stalled. "I just wondered if I could talk to you for a few minutes about Jim Cleary."

"Well, sure, honey. Pull up a desk. Is everything going OK on the campaign?"

Autumn sat down in one of the student desks. Mrs. Moore tried as gracefully as possible to fit her ample frame into the desk next to Autumn.

"Everything's going fine on the campaign. Jim's gaining in the polls, and it looks like he's got a good chance of winning," Autumn relayed.

"But?" the teacher prompted.

"But some things have happened that I'm a little uncomfortable with. And I can't decide if I should stay on his staff," Autumn concluded.

Mrs. Moore took on a motherly tone and looked seriously at the girl seated next to her. "What kinds of *things*, Autumn?"

"Just the way he looks at me—a lot. And a couple of times he's hugged me or rubbed my shoulder in a way that's a little more than friendly. . . ."

Mrs. Moore nodded, listening intently.

I'm afraid he might kiss me."

"KISS you?" Mrs. Moore almost flew out of her seat. "If he does, you tell me immediately and I'll go to the authorities."

"Oh, no, you can't do that." Autumn clenched her hands and stared at them. "Mrs. Moore, I'm afraid that I'm crazy and making all this up. I think I'm exaggerating it all."

Mrs. Moore reached over and touched Autumn's hand. "Tell me exactly what has happened."

Autumn traced the initials carved into the desk while she told Mrs. Moore about everything—except the kiss. ". . . so you see, it's all my fault—"

"All your fault? Honey! He's a grown man, for heaven's sake!"

"I know," Autumn said as she fought back tears, "but I have to admit, I did find him attractive, so maybe I made him think it was OK."

"Autumn, first of all you are not crazy. I don't think you are reading anything into what he is doing. AND what that man is doing is both unethical and close to being illegal. I don't care if you threw yourself across his desk, he still should have known better. Has he ever made any of these advances toward you in front of anyone else?"

"Well, no, we're always alone when—"

"See! That's exactly what I mean!" Mrs. Moore interrupted. "He knows good and well that what he's doing is wrong; otherwise, why would he be so secretive about it? That man is abusing his position."

Autumn sighed. These were words she didn't want to hear. "I guess you're right, Mrs. Moore."

"Well, if you wish, I'd be more than happy to go down there and give him a piece of this voter's mind!" Mrs. Moore vehemently offered.

Autumn stood up to leave. "I know you would. And I appreciate it. But I think I'd rather try to handle this myself first."

"Do you think that's wise?" Mrs. Moore asked. "You are still vulnerable. And if you are doubting that his actions are deliberate and a come-on, I'm not certain you can stand up to him."

"Aren't you the one who has taught me to stand up to the opposition?" Autumn asked.

"You *are* my best debate student. If you handle yourself with him the same way you do on the debate floor, I have no doubt you'll do just fine," Mrs. Moore said as she hugged her tightly.

*I wish I was as sure of that as you are,* thought Autumn.

Autumn tried to tame the nervousness she felt as she pulled into Cleary's office-turned-campaign-headquarters. As she drove in from school, she thought about the implications and the questions that would be raised if she simply dropped out. She knew she was too truthful to say nothing. And Cleary's magnetism and the incredible opportunities that she received by remaining on the team proved too powerful to ignore.

As she walked into the office, she saw the staff meeting to discuss the commercial spots that a local marketing agency had put together. Cleary's face lit up when he noticed her arrival.

"Hey, Autumn. Impeccable timing, girl. You won't believe this. It is a true piece of work. I think you'll recognize a lot of yourself in the TV ad."

Jan Crier, Cleary's administrative assistant slipped the tape in and the eight staff and volunteers quietly focused in on the TV monitor. Cleary didn't lie. The marketing firm had used her words throughout the thirty-second ad. At the end of it, everyone spontaneously cheered.

"All within budget, folks," Cleary said proudly. "All within budget. This should add even more momentum."

"I've got more good news," a young staffer announced. "The polls are in, and we're fifteen points ahead of Lindsay!" More applause.

Cleary raised his hand for silence. "The election isn't won yet. I want us to spend at least an hour dissecting this spot. Put yourself in the shoes of the voters. How will this sound to the Democrats, the elderly, the boomers, the busters?" Cleary said.

The team spent the next ninety minutes debating the emotional impact of the ad. Finally Cleary wrapped up the meeting.

"This is all we can do. Looks like it passes our litmus test. Now we've got the three focus groups coming in tomorrow, and then we'll really see how well we did. Let's get back to work. And Autumn, I'd like to discuss another strategy with you. Could you come back to my office?"

"Sure," Autumn said awkwardly.

Autumn followed Cleary into his office. He closed the door and sat down behind his mahogany desk and gestured for her to sit down. She could feel the slight tremble of her hand. This was the first time they had been together alone since the kissing fiasco.

"So . . . what's the strategy?" Autumn asked with a forced smile.

"I lied," Cleary said sincerely.

"You lied? About what?" Autumn asked.

"I lied about my ability to treat you like just another staff member. I can't do that," he said.

"Fine, I'll resign," Autumn said.

"You don't have to," Cleary replied.

"I don't want to be a distraction to you. I believe in what you are trying to do. I feel strongly that you should be our next leader and—"

Cleary interrupted her as he stood to his feet. "Autumn, you are not a distraction to me. That's not why I called you in here. I don't understand every single dynamic that comes into play here, but you give me a sense of power that I've never had before. You're so attractive and intelligent, and you have such an incredible future." Cleary looked as if tears were in his eyes, and he moved away from his desk and knelt by her chair. "I need you. I'm attracted to you, and I don't think there is anything wrong with telling you that."

"Jim, how can you say that? Can you imagine how the public will perceive it?" Autumn said.

"They'll never have to know, Autumn," Cleary said.

"I can't believe that you're doing this," Autumn said trembling from the panorama of emotions she felt.

"No one needs to know. No one *should* know. Autumn, there's a bond between us that you can't deny. I've felt it strongly ever since that time you stood up in that town-hall meeting. You were extraordinary. And the more I know about you, the more amazed I am that you are in my life. Your presence . . . it . . . well . . . it consumes me."

Cleary reached over and grabbed her hand softly.

"It's wrong," Autumn whispered as she fought her own desires.

"No it isn't. I'm not married."

"That still doesn't make it right," Autumn said. "I'm just a girl."

"No. I don't think you're just a girl," he said.

"Well, I am," Autumn said louder. "And that *is* an important element, or you wouldn't be keeping this secret."

Cleary drew his hand up to her face and caressed her cheek as a tear rolled down her face.

Finally she rallied her conscience and stood up. "You promised me that this would never happen."

"I'm sorry," Cleary said softly.

"I'm sorry too. I resign."

Autumn grabbed her briefcase and tried to mask her emotions as she walked out of the office. She unlocked the car door, sat down in the driver's seat, and rested her head on the steering wheel, heaving deep sobs and wondering why her world had suddenly fallen apart.

As Kandi had predicted, the change to friendship with Justin was awkward and painful. She had seen Justin twice at school. They both wore their best masks of stability and serenity, but they also did their best to avoid each other. She took alternate routes to her classes just to keep from seeing him. *How long will this last?* she wondered. She thought about calling him, but what would she say? So much had come between them now.

Kandi's mom walked in from work. When she saw her daughter's face, she dove straight into the subject. "So it's over."

"What?"

"You and Justin," Mrs. Roper clarified.

"You judge for yourself. You heard everything," Kandi replied.

"That's so sad. Justin has done so much for you," Mrs. Roper said.

"Are you *intentionally* trying to make me feel bad?" Kandi cried.

"I'm sorry. No, I just hope you'll still be friends."

"You and everybody I know," Kandi said.

"So does Zack have anything to do with this?"

"Zack is just a friend. I think. I don't know. He's just so exciting. I never know what will happen next. I enjoy being around him. He's funny. And impulsive and—"

"Just like your dad," Mrs. Roper replied.

"That's not why I like him, Mom. Believe me, I'd rather die than marry a guy like Dad."

"But you have to admit there are lots of similarities."

"But I'm not dating him," Kandi said assertively.

"Oh, really?" Mrs. Roper's face registered skepticism.

"Really, Mom. At least not now."

"Just remember: never say never," Mrs. Roper said as she walked to her bedroom.

As much as she hated to admit it, Kandi's attraction to Zack was growing. Was it some Freudian psychobabble impulse that drew her to Zack? She shuddered at the thought as she sat down at her computer and keyed in her Internet password. She opened her mailbox and found a note from Zack.

*Hey Kandi,*

*I hated to miss out on school. I really wanted to see you today. But going to school five straight days is against my religion. Gave it up for lent. What I want lent for I'll never know. It's just annoying clothes-dryer residue.*

*But seriously, Kandi, I just want you to know that I am extremely grateful to be your friend or whatever we are. I know it has been a stretch for you. Especially after the water-balloon incident and the library-stalking accusations. However, I think those incidents just show that I'm persistent.*

*No joke,* Kandi thought as she smiled at the screen.

*If you're trying to avoid me, giving me your E-mail address was absolutely the wrong thing to do. I'm addicted to E-mail. Close friends have accused me of spamming them with personal notes.*

*I know you are really into Christianity, and I just wanted to apologize if I sounded like I was mocking you at the cemetery the other day. I really wasn't. I just believe if you don't fully understand something, then what the heck—make fun of it. That's kinda how I deal with stuff like that. It usually comes across like I'm some sort of pompous jerk. Jerk—maybe. Pompous—no. I admit that Christianity might work for you, but I don't exactly understand all the faith business. I'm kind of a sight guy myself. I like to see things before I believe it. When I was a kid, I used to sit out in the middle of a field on my Grandpa's farm and scream up into the clouds: "GOD! SHOW YOURSELF! I'M WAITING! COME ON, GOD!"*

*Due to the fact that I'm not a TV evangelist, you may have guessed that God didn't show up. He wasn't there. But like you said on our way home Saturday—faith is not seeing. I just am a veritable plethora of questions when it comes to God.*

*"Why suffering? Why Hitler? Why war? Why AIDS? Yada, yada, yada . . . ."*

*I don't know if I'll ever find the answers to those questions but I think you might have some insight, some Joan of Arc revelation that you could let me in on. I'm open to it, and I promise I won't be such a closed-minded agnostic.*

Kandi clicked the reply button and stared at the empty memo. She searched the deep recesses of her mind for clues from all the Bible studies and books she had read in the past few months, but she couldn't put together a single complete sentence. She whispered a prayer for the right time and the right words to talk to Zack about her faith and then heard the familiar goodbye from her online service.

After Autumn left James Cleary's office, she drove around town trying to gain composure before facing her sometimes overly concerned parents. She tried to think of ways to word her sudden lack of interest in the campaign without implicating herself as a victim of a very messy ordeal. Every time she rehearsed explaining it to her parents, she worried they might feel she provoked or even nurtured the romance. "Maybe I did," she said to herself in the car. "Maybe I'm too blind to realize that my eyes *did* light up when I talked politics with a man who might run for president in ten years or so. Have I been too blind to see my own part in this?" Finally, after an hour, she arrived at her house. She took one long look in the rearview mirror and then with a deep breath to build confidence, she walked into the house.

"I'm back," she called out.

"And where have you been?" Rev. Sanders asked.

"Do you want the long version or the short version?" Autumn asked.

"I'd better settle for the short one right now because I have a feeling James Cleary will be calling to talk to you in a matter of seconds."

"Why?" Autumn asked.

"The man must want something from you because he's called three times in the past thirty minutes. He's a persistent man. What do you have that he wants?"

Autumn became dizzy trying to respond to that question.

"Autumn! Don't take it so seriously. I'm just amazed at how you've made yourself so indispensable to this future senator."

Autumn was relieved when the phone rang and even more relieved when her father promptly left the room to let her answer it.

"Hello?"

"Autumn, where did you go?" Cleary said in a soft concerned voice.

"I've just been driving around, wondering what I did to leave you so ethically bankrupt!" she said in quiet, angry tone.

"I'm sorry. I don't know. It's just getting so close to D-Day. I've just been a little crazy, I guess."

They were both silent for a moment.

"Autumn, I'm sorry. I need you. People have a connection with you that they don't have with me."

"I told you—I'm out, Jim."

"I'm asking you to reconsider, please," Cleary begged. "It's totally irrational for you to make this kind of rash decision."

"It is definitely not rash. I've been thinking about this

since—" Autumn stopped and glanced around to confirm confidentiality. "Since the first incident."

"You make it sound like I did this a hundred times," Cleary said.

"Twice is plenty for me," Autumn said.

"A few weeks. I'm only asking for a few weeks."

"A few seconds is too long," Autumn said with mature calmness.

"I can make it worth your while, I promise. Look, Autumn, you have been, I mean you still are, a star on my team, and I will reward you for your work."

"What do you mean?"

Cleary chuckled and said, "We are way above our financial goals for this campaign. You're worth more than any airtime I buy. That's a fact. If you stay on, I'll reward you with a sizable bonus. Ten thousand dollars if we win."

Autumn said nothing at first as the figure bounced around in her head. "What are you saying?" she finally responded.

"I mean it. Ten thousand dollars if you stay through the election and we win."

"I don't know," Autumn said hesitantly.

"Sleep on it, and I'll call you in the morning."

Click. Cleary was gone without a goodbye.

As Autumn held the phone in her hand, a flood of emotion swept through her consciousness. As strange as it seemed, she was still attracted to this dynamic man, and it had nothing to do with the money. She felt that she desperately needed him and wished she were twenty-one and not a teenager. What would it have been like if that were the situation?

"So what's up, Autumn?" Rev. Sanders asked.

"I don't think I can talk about it right now," Autumn said, trying to hide her face as he walked over and wrapped his arms around her, but in the circle of his arms, she began to weep.

"What is it, baby?" Rev. Sanders said sweetly.

"I don't think I can do this job anymore. I just don't think I'm being true to myself by doing it."

"Why?"

"It's different, Daddy. I'm sorry, Daddy. I really wanted to make you and Mom proud of me. I saw how proud you were of me. You showed that news clip to practically everyone who came into the church office."

"Hey, now, wait one second. I'm proud of you no matter what. There's nothing you could do to make me love you any more than I do. You know that, don't you?"

"I do. I guess I needed to hear you say that. I'm still not sure what to do. Cleary has offered me a ten-thousand-dollar bonus to stay on the team through the election," Autumn remarked.

Rev. Sanders looked down at his little girl with a furrowed brow. "Ten thousand dollars? Why?" her dad asked. "What's going on?"

"Nothing yet, Dad. He's just making me feel uncomfortable."

"I don't at all want to sound like I'm slighting your value, but ten grand is a lot of money for a few weeks more work." Autumn's dad paused but she knew his mind was in high gear. "Is the difference political? Or is it something else? Is he in trouble? Do you know something I don't?"

"You've always told me that our futures are determined . . ."

". . . by the friends we choose," her dad said, completing her sentence.

"I'm having trouble seeing myself walking down this kind of road—at least not now."

Autumn's dad looked deeply into her eyes, trying to grasp the meaning of her philosophical replies. "After this is all over, you promise me that you'll tell me the whole story."

"I will. Thanks, Daddy," Autumn said as she reached up to hug his tall frame.

"What for?"

"For trusting me," Autumn replied.

"One hundred percent," Rev. Sanders whispered into his daughter's ear.

Friday morning more than forty students met in the band room to discuss the recent threats on churches if Summit participated in the "See You at the Pole" event. A heaviness filled the room as they all found a place to sit. Usually the beginnings of these Fellowship of Christian Students meetings were filled with loud music and lots of laughter and excitement. But the threats, rumors, and speculation left them subdued and confused.

"We've had five threats," reported Luke Ellis, FCS president. "Two E-mails, two notes, and one phone call."

"So, were they all pretty much the same—threatening to burn a church if we pray Wednesday?" a student asked.

"Not burn," Justin replied. "They never said anything about burning. The notes just say they're going down."

"What do the police say?" another student asked.

"They're taking it seriously. I'd imagine it'd be easier if these guys threatened the school. But a church? There are hundreds of churches that they could target," Luke said.

"So what do we do now?" Luke asked the crowd. "We have to make a decision about this. We've got to meet with Jarvis and maybe even the police about whether we'll go ahead and take a chance that this is just a hoax, or just maybe pray somewhere else."

"I say it's a go," Clipper said with a strong determined voice. "We can't let these cowards run our school. We can't let them run our lives! I am so sick of the whole mess," Clipper said.

"Then why do you hang out with them?" a freshman guy asked.

"What?" Clipper asked, astonished.

"It's guys like A. C. that are doing this. Don't you see that? Jerks like him. Seems like you're talking out of both sides of your mouth."

"He's not involved, Clint," Clipper said firmly.

"How do you know?" the student countered.

"I asked him," Clipper replied.

"And you really think he'd tell you the truth?"

"I do," Clipper responded. "That's the reason we can't get guys like A. C. to come to our meetings. People think that just because he dyes his hair and wears leather that he's a felon. And you guys wonder why we can't grow," Clipper said in exasperation.

"Clipper," Justin said. "Chill, OK? Clint's not the enemy."

"I'm sorry. I'm just a little freaked out," Clipper said. "Listen. I know everyone else is freaking out about all of this too. I think we should go ahead with 'See You at the Pole.' If they threatened to shoot at the students as we gathered, I'd still be for praying. It's a national event, and I don't want to think when I'm fifty or so that we let some weird kook run this place." Clipper stood up and grabbed his backpack. "I've got to go. You know where I stand on this issue."

Autumn followed him out. "Clipper, wait up! What are you doing?"

"I don't know. It seems I can't go anywhere without people thinking I'm some sort of radical freak," Clipper said without turning around.

"This is not the way to solve problems. What good is it for you to just blow up and walk out? That is so cowardly," Autumn said.

"Cowardly?! You're calling me cowardly. What about them? What about the way *they* are acting?" Clipper said, finally stopping to face Autumn.

"They're scared. We all are. This isn't just about being some kind of martyr. Maybe you're right, but remember about what's happened in the past year. The violence in schools, bomb threats, the hurt and frightened students. I'm not sold on us canceling 'See You at the Pole' either. I just think we need to be a little more considerate of other people's fears."

Suddenly the door to the band room opened, and Justin quietly left the room. He walked over to Autumn and Clipper.

"So what's the deal?" Autumn asked.

"We took a vote right after you two left," Justin said. "Twenty-eight to five in favor of participating. I just hope we're right."

Later that same morning, Luke and Justin met in the school office at the request of Summit's principal, Ms. Jarvis. Although she didn't state the purpose of the meeting, they were sure it involved "See You at the Pole," which was coming up Wednesday morning.

After everyone had taken a seat, Ms. Jarvis began. "I don't enjoy these kinds of decisions. But we've got to take these threats seriously. We've gotten the same threat that you received a few days ago. The note said that a church would be bombed if Summit High students insisted on praying around the flagpole Wednesday morning."

"How many threats?" Justin asked.

"Three other people reported threats, and someone had the gall to fax in one from a library across town. Are you still planning to participate?"

"Ms. Jarvis," Luke began, "It's not like we came up with the idea. It's a national event."

"I understand that. I'm asking you to look beyond your own desires. There are other people to be considered," Ms. Jarvis said in a motherly tone.

"Don't you see what that says to whoever's making the threats. It says they can just push us around and make us run," Justin said.

"I don't think the churches would agree with you. They are all just as frightened as I am about this. And it is my duty as a community leader to consider their needs. Frankly, Justin, knowing you as I do, I'm surprised that you don't really seem to care."

"I do care, Ms. Jarvis. I care deeply. It could be *my* church that goes down, but I still think you're punishing us and not thinking about the real adversary."

Luke interrupted, "Maybe she's right, Justin."

"What?" Justin said as he looked over at Luke, surprised by his sudden conclusion. "I thought you—"

"I'm just saying that there's a lot of risk involved in this," Luke said.

"I thought you were going to represent the FCS and the vote we took," Justin said to Luke.

"As the president of the club, I'm not sure this is the right thing to do."

"That settles it for me," Ms. Jarvis said as she closed her day planner and stood up.

"Settles what?" Justin asked.

"I'll announce at the school board meeting Monday night that the FCS leadership has decided to cease its participation in this event until we are certain that the threats are no longer viable."

"But that's not what we decided," Justin said in shock.

Luke chimed in, "Wait, Ms. Jarvis. I only meant that maybe we should reconsider."

"When it comes to safety, I must take the lead," Ms. Jarvis said. "Good day."

That afternoon Clipper sat down on the couch in his living room prepared to face his parents' decision about whether they would let him return to Louisville to see Jenny. They had seemed hesitant when he proposed the trip a few days ago and had not given him permission.

"Your mother and I," Mr. Hayes began (it was always an omen when Clipper's father began this way), "are concerned about this whole situation. We think Jenny's a wonderful girl, and we think her parents are treating her unfairly. It's none of our business, but that's the way we feel. And we have concerns about what you're thinking right now, and about this trip you want to make."

"If you want to know what I'm thinking, I'm thinking that Jenny is scared. I'm thinking that she doesn't have anyone there supporting her. And now she's even in the hospital. She might lose the baby. She needs someone," Clipper said in machine-gun speed.

"We know all that," Mr. Hayes said with understanding.

His mother spoke. "I guess a big part of our fear is that she might be relying on you so much that you might make a choice that could affect the rest of your life."

Clipper's heart sank. Now he knew they feared the thing that had already occurred. He looked for further clarification as his head began to pound with tension.

Clipper's father's eyes scanned the living room as he searched for the right words to say. "I guess—I mean, what we're trying to say is . . . " A long awkward pause preceded his next statement, "Clipper, you've got the biggest heart of any kid we know. There's nobody that'll make the kind of sacrifices you'd make for others. You'd fight lions for your friends. That's a great trait. It's a godly trait. The only thing about it is that lots of times you'll help people without thinking of your own well-being. We just don't want to see you make a mistake."

Clipper tried his best to not appear angry by the sudden change to a father/son sermon. He knew his dad was right. But at the moment, he just wanted a yes or no. "So can I go?"

"Are you listening to what we're saying?" Clipper's mom asked.

Clipper nodded with arms crossed defensively.

Mr. Hayes rolled his eyes and smiled. "We'll let you go. But we want Shawn to go with you." Clipper wasn't surprised that Shawn, the youth minister at their church, was his parents' choice.

"That's fine," Clipper said. "I don't care if you want Mister Rogers to go as my chaperone. I just have to get down there."

Clipper left the family meeting elated that he'd be allowed to go but also experiencing a touch of guilt that he withheld his greatest struggle from them: He'd already told Jenny he'd make that commitment. Now that he'd made a lifelong commitment to Jenny, could he go through with it?

# 29

Autumn didn't call James Cleary for two days, and he didn't attempt to call her. Her confusion continued to mount. This opportunity had accelerated into something most young people would only dream about. She had proved herself to be a vital member of a winning campaign effort. She would have the opportunity to be an agent of change. She found Jim's magnetic personality and quick analytical mind fascinating, and yet she felt ashamed. She also imagined all the things she would be able to do with ten thousand dollars. In a matter of one month, she would earn more money than her father made in three. Her prayers seemed to hit the ceiling and fall back on the bed where she laid. The privacy of the quandary grew even more painful as the hours passed. She knew she had to make a decision. As she replayed her moment of triumph and shame, she sat up and looked at the phone by her bed. Impulsively, she dialed Eli's number.

"Hello?"

"Eli?"

"Yes?"

"I just had to call you," Autumn said, fighting back her tears.

"Autumn? That you?"

Autumn tried to laugh, "I know. Weird, huh?"

"Yes. A little weird. Especially after the hang-up this week," Eli said. "You sound different."

"I'm just tired."

"No, it sounds like you're shook up or something," Eli said.

"I just wanted to call and tell you . . ." Autumn paused, wiped her eyes, angry that her emotions were so out of control.

"Tell me what?" Eli said, filling the dead air.

"Just to tell you that I'm sorry," Autumn said.

"Really? Could you repeat that?" Eli said, sounding as if he were toying with her.

"You really like this, don't you?"

"What?" Eli said.

"You really like hearing me say that I'm sorry," Autumn said.

"I'm just shocked. You were the last person I expected to call. I didn't think you had any inclination whatsoever to even see my face," Eli replied.

"I know. I was a jerk," Autumn said honestly.

"I just figured that you had lots of issues, you know. And that you really didn't want to deal with someone who told you that you were a workaholic. Basically that's what I called you, and you had every right to click on me."

"Click?" Autumn asked

"You know. Hang up."

"You're right. I do have a lot of issues. That is true. Still do.
I feel like I've been carrying the weight of the entire world. I'm
too young for this. I started thinking about my life, and I can't
remember the last time I just had a great time just doing something for fun. No matter where I go, it seems like I've got to
have an agenda," Autumn said as she paced her room with the
cordless.

"I'll have to agree with you there," Eli said.

"I don't even know how to rest anymore. In fact, I don't
even have time to rest or just sit down and talk to God. I feel
like such a hypocrite."

"I think we all struggle with our prayer life," Eli said.

"But it's much deeper than that," Autumn said.

"Like what?"

"I'm facing the toughest decision I've ever faced in my life.
It's like I've come to a fork in the road, and I have to decide
what I'm going to do. The tough part is that the easiest choice
is going to be the wrong one."

"That's common," Eli said. "Enter through the narrow gate.
For wide is the gate and broad the road that leads to destruction."

"Wow, I'm impressed," Autumn said, astounded by the sudden biblical reference.

"Do you want to talk about it? I mean, all you've told me so
far is that you are busy, depressed, confused, flustered, and sorry."

Autumn couldn't help laughing.

"Really. Why don't we meet somewhere and talk about it,"
Eli said.

"I don't think I'm ready to do that. I just wanted to tell you that I'm sorry," Autumn said.

"Forgiven," Eli said immediately.

"Really?" Autumn asked skeptically.

"Come on, Autumn. Don't act surprised."

"Thanks, Eli. I just need you to be patient with me right now," Autumn said.

"Sure. No problem. I can handle that," Eli said matter-of-factly.

"Thanks. I'll get back with you," Autumn said.

"Autumn?" Eli said.

"Yes?"

"I'm here if you need anything."

"I know."

Shawn drove into Clipper's driveway Saturday morning. Clipper hopped into the car, and they headed to Louisville. It was all small talk for an hour. Finally Shawn asked the question, "So what's up with Jenny?"

"She's been in and out of the hospital for the past few days. Eclampsia. Have you ever heard of that?" Clipper asked.

"No. Can't say that I have."

"She doesn't really have anyone. Her parents are acting like jerks. You know, I really liked them when we first met. They were really cool. But can you imagine just shipping your daughter out of town because she's pregnant? I mean, if there's one time in her life that she needs someone in her corner, it's now. And it's like they just checked out."

"Some parents do that. So where do you fit in?" Shawn asked.

"I haven't figured that one out yet," Clipper said.

"I'm sure she's looking for someone to be beside her through all this," Shawn said.

"I'm the one," Clipper said immediately.

"For how long?"

"As long as it takes," Clipper said, staring straight ahead.

After a mile of silence Shawn asked, "You love her?"

"I do."

More silence.

"Did I ever tell you that I almost got married before I moved to Indy?" Shawn asked.

"No, I think I missed that one," Clipper said.

"I did. Her name was Lisha. We got engaged when I was still in college. I really thought she was the one. With a capital O," Shawn said.

"What happened?"

"It's hard to say. Her grandmother, who practically raised her since she was five, died of cancer right before we met. I really felt like Lisha was in love with me and that I loved her, but after a while, there was a gap there."

Clipper looked over at him, puzzled. "What do you mean a gap?"

"I don't know exactly. I guess the best way to describe it is that when I met her, she had lots of needs, and I was glad to fill those needs. She needed companionship and friendship. Hey, I can be a great friend. She needed someone to take care of her during the crisis. Great, I thought. That's my gift. But the more she healed, the more distant we became. Probably the toughest thing I've ever had to face was facing the fact that as people heal, they're different than when they're wounded and need love."

"OK, give it up. Did Dad tell you to give me the talk?" Clipper asked.

"Nope. I don't talk for other people. I'm talking to you as a friend and an older brother. Maybe I'm way off base, Clipper. But I love you. You know that. I just want you to make sure that you really pray about what your relationship is and what it's going to become. I'd hate for you to wake up two years from now—in college, married, and wondering who that person is that's sleeping next to you in the two-room apartment three blocks from the university. That almost happened to me."

They were both silent and thoughtful. Clipper looked out the window as they listened to Shawn's stereo, every now and then making small talk. They didn't return to the subject of marriage the rest of the morning, but Shawn's words kept running through Clipper's head. The youth minister's comments made Clipper wonder what life would be like two years from this day. He felt as if his destiny would be found in the conversation he would have with Jenny.

*What will I say?* he wondered. *If I change my mind and back out, would I lose the relationship all together? What was the driving motivation for a relationship with her? Is it just a desire to be a Superman? To solve her problems? To shelter her from her personal storms? Is it hormones? Is it infatuation? How will I ever know? Lord, You've got to show me,* he prayed silently.

Kandi and Eli came over to Autumn's house early that evening. It was the first time in a long time they'd had the chance to just sit around and visit. Autumn's parents had gone to a concert downtown. Rev. Sanders presented the ground rules as only he could in his deep bass voice. "No weird stuff, no other kids, no parties . . . "

"Honey!" Autumn's mom chimed in. "Who do you think she is? It's Autumn, for goodness sake."

"I know. I've got to act a little paranoid. Isn't that what fatherhood is all about?"

"Have fun, kids. We'll be back. Please clean up after Hootie and the Blowfish leave," she said.

"Hootie and the what?" Rev. Sanders said seriously.

"It's a band. Just a joke. Now, let's go."

Shortly after they left, Kandi asked the question she had been dying to ask since she got there. "So, what happened? Why did you give it up?"

"I think you know the answer to that question, Kandi."

"He kept on?" Kandi asked.

"'Till the bitter end," Eli said.

"Let me get this straight. You told Eli the whole deal, but you haven't told me?" Kandi said.

"He just happened to ask first," Autumn said.

"Some guys can be so yucky," Eli said in a fake effeminate voice.

"I hate when you do that, Eli," Autumn said.

"So give me the lowdown, Autumn," Kandi demanded.

"The story is pretty straightforward. I really prayed about it. I knew I only had a few weeks more to put up with him, and he offered me a pretty astounding bonus. But the more I tried to convince myself that I could stick it out until the election, the more I disliked myself. I just couldn't respect myself if I sacrificed who I was for money or power or anything. So I just wrote him a letter and slipped it under the door earlier today. I said I enjoyed the opportunity that he gave me, and I said thanks, but no thanks. Best of luck."

"That's all?" Kandi asked. "Did he call you or try to get in touch with you?"

"No. I really wouldn't expect him to. I've said no to him three times in the past few days. It might just damage his poor ego if he got turned down by a young girl again."

The doorbell rang, and Kandi went to the door and peered through the eyehole. "Oh, great . . ." Kandi said with a twinge of defensiveness in her voice.

"What? Who is it?" Autumn said.

"Cleary," Kandi replied.

"James Cleary is here?" Eli said as he stood up from the table to his feet.

"The one and only," Kandi said.

"Look guys. I'll handle this," Autumn said calmly. "Why don't you go into Dad's study."

"I don't think that's really a good idea," Eli said.

"I can handle it!" Autumn said with her jaw set.

Eli and Kandi slipped into the office that was adjacent the living room.

"Just do something obvious if he gets weird on you," Eli said softly.

"Like scream 'murder'," Kandi said as she closed the door.

Autumn rolled her eyes and walked to the door as the doorbell rang once again.

"Hello, Autumn," Cleary said seriously.

"I assume you didn't get my note," Autumn said as her heart rate accelerated.

"Oh, I got it all right. Can't say I completely understand you," Cleary said.

"Understand me? I'm not asking you to understand me. I just want you to respect my—"

"Sorry. I can't respect you. You are bailing out on the campaign in the heat of battle," Cleary said.

"You should have thought about that before you decided to keep making passes at me," Autumn said, suddenly feeling very calm.

"You enjoyed it, Autumn. Don't lie about it. You liked it," Cleary said.

"It doesn't matter whether I did or not. It's still unethical and illegal," Autumn said.

"What did I ever do to you that made you so disenchanted with me?"

"Where do I begin, Cleary?" Autumn said, backing away from him.

"I hate it when you call me Cleary. My name is Jim."

"I prefer calling you Cleary," Autumn said louder.

"You're a fool. Do you know the places I could have taken you? Do you have any idea of the opportunities you're losing?"

"I know," Autumn said.

"Then why?" Cleary asked.

"Opportunities come and go. This opportunity is going right out the door. Please," Autumn said.

"A good-bye kiss?" Cleary said.

"No," Autumn said assertively.

Cleary approached her and whispered, "I can make your dreams come true, Autumn. You know I can. Give in. It'll be worth it."

The study door swung open quickly, and Eli strode out. "Are you deaf? She said no. Who do you think you are?"

"Who are *you?*" Cleary said, sounding trapped and nervous.

"Get out," Autumn said.

"I don't have to listen to some punk hiding in a room to tell me when and where I go. You are way out of your league, kid," Cleary said.

Eli stood his ground. "Out of *my* league? You were out of your league when you walked into this house."

Cleary looked over to Autumn and said, "I never knew you had a brother."

"He's not my brother," Autumn said. Her mind raced as she tried to think of what to say next. Her logical mind scanned the implications of her impulse but she blurted it out anyway. "He's my boyfriend."

Eli looked as surprised as Cleary at the sudden announcement.

They spent a few moments staring at each other waiting for someone to break the tense silence. Finally Eli spoke up, "I'd suggest you leave."

"I don't have to take orders from a smart-mouth punk," Cleary said.

"You're going to regret you said that," Eli said uncrossing his arms and strengthening his stance.

"It's all in who you know," Cleary said as he started toward the door.

"That's right. Do you know Thomas Nellon, district attorney?" Eli said.

"Yes, I do," Cleary said. "Why?"

"Just a cousin of mine. If only I had a tape of what I just heard while we were in the study. Maybe I do," Eli said, lifting a tape out of his back pocket.

"Keep your nose out of this. You don't know who you're dealing with," Cleary said angrily.

"Sounds like we're dealing with sexual harassment of a minor, unless you leave pretty dang quick," Eli said, stepping toward him.

Cleary's eyes scanned the three as he reached for the door and left without saying another word.

A few moments after Cleary left, Autumn looked at Eli with utter bewilderment. "What was that all about? You taped the conversation?"

Eli laughed and said, "Whoa! I didn't say that. I'm sorry. I'm not that fast. I just said *maybe* I taped it. Besides, do you think I'd tape over Jennifer Knapp? This," Eli said, waving the tape before their eyes, "was just a visual aid to show him what a cassette might look like *if* I had taped it."

"And what's this about Thomas Nellon?! I didn't know you were his cousin," Kandi said.

"Well, I am. But he's not like a first cousin. He's my dad's third cousin. Really!"

"Which makes you . . . " Autumn asked.

"Which makes us, well . . . pretty much strangers."

32

Clipper didn't tell Shawn about the letter or the decisions he faced. It scared him to think what Shawn might tell him if the youth minister knew Clip had told Jenny he'd marry her. He admitted it even sounded illogical when he stood in front of the mirror and practiced telling people. On the other hand, Clipper hated the dating scene, and he cared deeply for Jenny. This was the first time he'd had feelings like this. The feelings were in many ways intoxicating. His heart seemed to cry out for something permanent, something different. But how much would he have to sacrifice to be there?

They parked in the hospital parking lot around nightfall. Clipper felt like he would burst if he didn't come clean with Shawn. He began to cry.

"What is it, Clipper?" Shawn asked.

"I don't want to tell you this, but now I think I've *got* to tell you," Clipper said as they sat in the car with the engine still running.

"What is it?"

"I'm sorry. I should trust you. You've never done me wrong," Clipper replied.

"And I'm not going to. Clipper, you know that I'm not going to freak. I'm unfreakable," Shawn said with a smile.

"I guess I need to just let you read this," Clipper said as he pulled Jenny's letter out of his front pocket.

Shawn read the letter silently. Clipper couldn't believe that his friend could read it with a smile. "Wow," Shawn said. "Jenny is really taken by you, huh?"

"It'd be a lot easier if I didn't love her too," Clipper said.

"Sure."

"What are you going to do now?" Clipper asked.

"What am I gonna do? I think I'll help you find her, and then get some dinner in the cafeteria," Shawn said casually.

"That's it? No emergency calls to the Hayes family?"

"No."

"No sermons?"

"No," Shawn replied. "This is one of those things that you have to face by yourself. All I can do right now is pray for you. I can't force my opinions on you."

Clipper wiped his eyes and looked over at Shawn. "But you don't think I should do this."

"No. But I have to trust that God will give you an answer about what is right for you. He's got a plan for you, and I can't sit here and say that I know what that plan is," Shawn replied.

Clipper walked up to the door of Jenny's room alone and knocked quietly.

"Come in," Jenny said and smiled when she saw Clipper.

"Are you all right?" Clipper asked.

"I'm lots better than when I checked in," Jenny said.

"I've been so worried."

"You've been crying," Jenny said.

"Yes. As you know, I'm not very good with masks. I hoped I could be the strong one, but I guess I'm not," Clipper said as his eyes dropped to the floor.

"Just because you cry doesn't make you weak," Jenny said as he sat down on her bed and stroked her hair.

"Did I ever tell you how much you mean to me?" Clipper whispered.

Jenny's smile communicated that he had.

"But you can't go through with it," she said.

New tears pooled in the corners of his eyes as he shook his head.

"You're right. It wouldn't be fair to you," Jenny said softly.

"And it wouldn't be fair for you either. I want to be with you. I want to see you through all of this. But I'd hate for you to wake up one day and wonder if you married me out of convenience or just sheer panic," Clipper said.

"I guess I just needed to hear you say that," Jenny said. "You know, I've felt like I've been on a totally different planet. All alone. Without any hope that I could ever return. I've been reading this Bible that you sent me. I thought I'd never be caught dead reading the Bible. I've got a lot of questions to ask you."

"I've got plenty of time to answer them, Jenny," Clipper assured her. "Plenty of time."

The following Monday night, the largest crowd ever to attend a school board meeting packed into the large municipal conference room. Kandi, Autumn, and Clipper had been among the first to arrive.

"Where's Justin? I thought you said he would be here," Autumn asked Clipper.

"He's coming, but he said he'd be late. I think he's still ticked about Kandi."

Kandi jerked her head around and gave Clipper the eye. "Go ahead; blame it on me. It's all my fault," she said, folding her arms.

Suddenly Justin walked up from behind. "'Scuse me. This seat taken?" he asked, as if he were a stranger to the three.

"Doggone, speak of the devil," Clipper said with a smile.

"I'm sure I've been called worse," he replied. Justin looked over at Kandi and said, "And you, Kandi Roper, I'd like to talk to you after this is over."

Kandi looked surprised at the playfulness in his voice. "Sure," she replied. "I'll talk if you can give me a ride home."

"Hmmm . . . " Justin said, rubbing his chin. "I think I can fit that in. I'll have to change routes and so forth, but I guess so."

"So what are the odds they'll forbid prayer anywhere near the school on Wednesday?" Kandi asked, trying to divert attention away from the topic at hand.

"About 99.9 percent," Justin said. "Ms. Jarvis is adamant about it."

"Maybe so," Autumn said, "but that kind of ruling on an off-campus prayer meeting outside school hours is so unconstitutional that Jefferson, Lincoln, and Franklin will turn over in their graves simultaneously if the motion passes. If they think they can appease these weirdos by complying with these demands, they haven't learned much from history. They should know by now that you can't negotiate with terrorists, or you'll fall victim to their demands every time."

"Well spoken," Clipper said. "But save it for the figure-heads, will ya?"

The agenda of the meeting designated the "See You at the Pole" issue as the final item.

"Maybe they'll run out of time, and they won't have time to deal with the issue of banning it," Kandi said.

Autumn shook her head. "No way. They love visibility, and there are more cameras in this room than there were when they tried to implement uniforms for students."

"Now *that* was a cat fight," Clipper said smiling.

"Got that right," Justin said, scanning the room with his eyes.

The meeting droned on for ninety minutes as they addressed everything from twenty-five-year teaching anniversaries to rewriting policies on fund-raisers. Finally the moderator recognized Ms. Jarvis.

She stood at the podium and looked sternly at the audience. "I know that we have all been concerned for the safety of the churches of Indianapolis due to the threats we've received. The pastors of this community are very concerned; many are fearful of the impending fate of their beloved buildings. As of now, we've heard reports of over a dozen threats. All of them state in writing, in E-mails and faxes, and through very brief phone communications that a church will be destroyed if Summit High participates in the religious event 'See You at the Pole.' I would ask this body of educators to allow me the authority, for the sake of these churches, to deny any student access to the school and its property until the first bell. This would satisfy these lunatics and give us more time to investigate the threats that place these houses of worship in grave danger."

The superintendent of schools called for discussion. Several parents of students and teachers joined Jarvis in calling for the ban. Finally the superintendent gestured in the direction of Autumn and said, "And you have—"

"Yes, I do," Autumn said as she stood.

"Actually, Miss Sanders, I was recognizing the fellow next to you. The one with the unusual hair," he said, smiling at Clipper.

Clipper stood dumbfounded, pointing at himself, mouthing to the superintendent: *me?!*

"Go ahead," Justin whispered to Clipper.

"I was scratching my head," he said quietly.

Autumn said, "I'd like the opportunity to—"

"I'm sure you would. You've proven to be a master at debate, Miss Sanders. I was hoping to first hear from someone who is perhaps a little less schooled than you."

"Then you certainly have your man," Autumn said, smiling playfully at Clipper, followed by a wave of laughter. "Go for it."

Clipper stood in shock, looking back at Autumn, smiling and trying to put together a sentence.

"Well Mr., Sir, or should I say Doctor . . . or what?"

"Sir will be fine," the moderator said as he leaned into his microphone on the desk.

"You know. I was like . . . just . . . well, sitting here thinking. You know . . . thinking, well . . . "

"Go right ahead," the moderator said as he tried to move Clipper into complete sentences.

"I was just thinking that this kind of ruling on an outside prayer meeting before school starts is so unconstitutional that Jefferson, Lincoln, and Franklin would turn over in their graves simultaneously if it, you know . . . passes."

The audience reacted to the statement with a chorus of applause. Autumn just smiled and shook her head. Clipper's confidence blossomed along with his volume.

"And," he continued, "if you think we can appease these weirdos by complying with these demands, you haven't learned much from history." Now scattered cheers accompanied the applause.

Clipper held his hands up to ask for quiet, like a seasoned politician. His volume and intensity reached an even higher level as he pulled the hand-held microphone out of its stand. "Everyone should know by now that you can't negotiate with terrorists, or you'll fall victim to their demands every time."

The supporters of 'See You at the Pole' went crazy as Clipper reattached the microphone and returned to his seat, receiving high-fives from total strangers. Autumn just smiled, leaned over to Clipper, and whispered, "I didn't know you listened that well. In some states you can be sued for stealing intellectual property."

"Then sue away, girl," he said as he hugged her.

The superintendent addressed Autumn. "So, Ms. Sanders, I think you wanted to address the board."

"Sir, I believe I am at a loss for words," she said.

The superintendent stared above his bifocals, scanning the crowd. "Yes sir?" he said, as he spotted Rev. Sanders at one of the aisle microphones.

"I would like to respectfully correct Ms. Jarvis. Not all pastors are fearful of these attacks. I'm a pastor of an African-American congregation just a few miles east of here. I, for one, am not afraid of these threats. Now mind you, I doubt I'll be in our building on Wednesday morning, but I believe strongly that the church isn't bricks and mortar. It is flesh and blood. God does not dwell in buildings, so why should I be concerned?"

"Very gallant pronouncement, pastor. But I must confess I'm a bit skeptical about the number of pastors in this crowd who would agree with you. Many of them have called. I'm sure some have even recruited their members to be here."

"You may be right," Rev. Sanders said. "Are there any other pastors who feel we should stop this gathering?" he asked the crowd. "Please stand so that we may hear your side of the issue."

The challenge froze the assembly. Several men leaned forward as if they would stand, and yet they seemed to be unable to move. After a few moments, Rev. Sanders spoke into the microphone once more. "Are there any pastors who are in agreement with my position?" No one stood. Sanders' eyes surveyed the large room packed with people. Finally an old man stood in the back and said, "I'm Pastor Clebold. I've been a pastor of Parkview Presbyterian for thirty-five years. Can't believe I'm saying this. We aren't a large church, but I'd be more than happy to let them bomb our building if that's what it takes to keep kids praying."

One by one, pastors of all denominations and sizes stood in support of the students.

"It's really happening. I can't believe this," Autumn said under her breath.

"I hope we're doing the right thing," Justin replied.

The students in favor of "See You at the Pole" celebrated the victory with restraint, knowing that there could be dire consequences in less than forty-eight hours.

Tuesday night, A. C. lay in bed for more than four hours trying to erase the horrible nightmares he'd had all week about the bomb he had created. *Where did this conscience come from?* he asked himself.

At 5 A.M., he finally gave up on sleep and slipped out of the house. He drove down the interstate, departing from the lights of the city into suburbs and finally down a desolate road. An hour later he arrived at the place his friends called The Cave. It was simply a dilapidated storm shelter that the group had claimed as its own. It contained the basic equipment and supplies to build bombs. For a year The Association had schemed acts of violence. They reveled in the idea of inflicting citywide terror. It gave them a sense of power. Just as A. C. feared, the supplies and equipment had been removed from the cave.

He shined his flashlight around the empty room and opened a cabinet, which was attached to the wall of the musty shelter. He found the notebook where the group recorded their progress. It astounded A. C. that they'd leave it there. His heart pounded as he open the notebook and looked at the final entry.

*A. C. stricken. Rock and Roll Wednesday morning 7:30 at Book Three, New Testament.*

A. C. knew that "stricken" meant "death" to the group. He had been sentenced to die. Rock and Roll at Book Three, New Testament. *What is Book Three?* he asked himself. He ran back to his car and pulled from his glove compartment the green New Testament that Clipper had given him a few weeks before. A. C. had meant to throw it away many times, but he never did. Now he knew why. Book Three, New Testament. He turned to the contents page. His finger traveled down the page to the third entry. *The Gospel according to St. Luke.*

Time became A. C.'s greatest enemy as he sped back toward town. It was after 7 as he headed to St. Luke's Christian Church. His mind transported him to the scenes of Columbine High. The shock of the nation, the hatred of every parent and teacher. For the first time in his life, it seemed, he really cared. And he knew he had to get to the bomb in St. Luke's.

He flew through the deserted streets, his heart bouncing furiously off his rib cage. He knew the schedule. He had ten minutes left. As he turned into the church parking lot, he looked for any sign of people inside. It looked empty so far. As he got out of his car, he looked down the avenue and saw Elliot's Camaro fleeing the scene and wondered if he'd been seen. Probably not—otherwise, they would have turned around. Chances are The Association would have executed A. C. if they had caught him. Life was as cheap as garbage to Elliot, just as it used to be to A. C. But in the span of twenty-four hours, A. C. had become The Association's worst enemy.

He quickly, silently raced to the back entrance of the church and saw the scraps of a plastic bag and small strands of wire that Elliot had discarded carelessly. A. C. knew that the back entrance was the plan in all scenarios they had discussed. He reached for the doorknob. Locked. Elliot had the presence of mind to lock the door! He backed up and kicked the door, praying that the bomb sat further inside the building. He cracked the face of the door but it didn't open.

Once again, with even more anger and force, he kicked the door. The door flew open. The sudden high-pitched sound of the security system greeted A. C., adding even greater stress. At that moment he realized that the church's security system must been engaged when Elliot and company placed the bomb. This left him with even less time to do his work. The police would be on their way.

It was 7:27 A.M. A. C. knew three minutes stood between silence and a terrible explosion. He ran through the dark corridors of the small church, feeling his way through, tripping on the tables and chairs of the old neighborhood church.

Finally just ahead, he saw the familiar blinking red light. During their planning, Elliot and A. C. had often set the timer and imagined the detonation and chaos that would follow. He walked cautiously toward the bomb and peered into the LED clock. Three minutes left. Just as the note said. With trembling hands he searched the walls for a light switch. He turned the light on quickly and pulled the wire cutters out of the front pocket of his jeans. From his back pocket he pulled out the handwritten diagram Elliot had given him the week before.

"God, if you're out there, don't let this thing go off," he whispered under his breath. "Red, they're dead. Blues, you lose," he chanted three times as he tried to relax. It was the reminder Elliot had given him when A. C. was to help plant the bomb.

A. C. slowly moved the crude wire cutters closer to the blue wire. Forty-five seconds and counting. Slowly he applied pressure to the handle of the wire cutters and cut the wire. The clock stopped, and a split second later the LED screen went blank. A. C. ran for the door and tripped on a chair in the hall. His fall jammed his head into the corner of the doorframe. Dizzy, yet determined to flee, A. C. stumbled out the door and into the bright morning sun. He heard the approaching sirens and raced into the shadows.

Thanks for visiting Summit High. I'd love to hear from you
if you ever want to ask a question, swap stories,
need prayer, or even vent about life in general.
My E-mail address is mtullos@lifeway.com
See ya!
Matt Tullos